The Unencumbered Woman

Mary Alice Davies

Copyright © 2020 Mary Alice Davies

The moral right of the author has been asserted.

Apart from any fair dealing for the purposes of research or private study, or criticism or review, as permitted under the Copyright, Designs and Patents Act 1988, this publication may only be reproduced, stored or transmitted, in any form or by any means, with the prior permission in writing of the publishers, or in the case of reprographic reproduction in accordance with the terms of licences issued by the Copyright Licensing Agency. Enquiries concerning reproduction outside those terms should be sent to the publishers.

Matador
9 Priory Business Park,
Wistow Road, Kibworth Beauchamp,
Leicestershire. LE8 0RX
Tel: 0116 279 2299
Email: books@troubador.co.uk
Web: www.troubador.co.uk/matador
Twitter: @matadorbooks

ISBN 978 183859 258 5

British Library Cataloguing in Publication Data.
A catalogue record for this book is available from the British Library.

Printed and bound in Great Britain by 4edge Limited
Typeset in 10pt Sabon by Troubador Publishing Ltd, Leicester, UK

Matador is an imprint of Troubador Publishing Ltd

The Unencumbered Woman

*To the women, and men, who struggle with
the challenge of being unencumbered.*

Contents

Where are the women!   1

Rebooting intimacy   2

The dilemma of owning yourself   12

Revenge is sweet!   19

The Flying Club   34

The living in la-la land mission   41

Twice as much husband and half as much money   52

The scent of hope   62

The unencumbered woman   79

Where are the Women!

Shame
They're not on the board.
Because they don't fall on their sword?
They're not in the club.
Because they can't afford the sub?
They're not in the House.
Playing second fiddle to their spouse?
They don't control the bank.
It doesn't do to be too frank?
We know that this is wrong.
Women are bold, clever and strong.
For society it's a shame.
More women would raise the game.
Women should have more power.
We could get rid of the old shower,
An elite of Oxbridge men,
Living ordinary lives, really, when?
So know nothing of the strain
Women go through to obtain,
Work, respect, power and the right
To dignity and a chance to see their light
Shine.

Rebooting Intimacy

When the flat was empty of other people, Sam turned on the computer to check the progress of the delivery. It had been carefully planned so that the parcel would arrive on Saturday morning while the flatmates were away for the weekend. The delivery was on track, expected at 8am the next day. Sam was too anxious to sleep well and was up by 7am just in case it arrived early. It didn't.

The shipment was from a warehouse in California supplied by a university known for innovation in robot technology. Sam was nervous and nearly severed a finger when cutting the string around the large parcel. There would be a lot of bubble wrap to dispose of. Sam gently removed the sexbot and gasped. She was beautiful, if not altogether humanoid. Rather too perfect for a mere mortal. Total customisation had been expensive so her features had been selected from an online catalogue, a more affordable option. She looked like Audrey Hepburn. Sam had always had a thing about Audrey Hepburn, ever since seeing her in *Funny Face*. Real women were too terrifying to approach so the sexbot was an expensive experiment. From the online catalogue of smells, Sam had chosen the perfume "Obsession". It was a very exotic smell, which unfortunately lingered. Sam began to think it might have been a bad decision. The flatmates might start asking questions.

Her technology was impressive as Sam began to find out. When touched she smiled, and she made soft sighing sounds when stroked. She couldn't stand up unaided but that was no problem because Sam wanted her lying down. The app had already arrived on Sam's laptop so there had been opportunity to study the instructions on how to make the most of Audrey, as Sam had decided to call her. She didn't talk, the technology for that was still a bit crude, but Sam remembered Audrey's voice from her films and with a vivid imagination no speech was needed. However, she groaned and grunted appreciatively when Sam touched her in certain places. It was going to be a fantastic weekend.

By Sunday afternoon, Sam had worked through Audrey's repertoire at least three times. Those techies in California certainly knew a thing or two about giving pleasure. Audrey had functions that Sam didn't even know existed. It was money well spent. Music made the experience feel more intimate. From memory, Audrey liked jazz in *Funny Face,* so that was what she got. Just as well that Sam liked jazz too.

There was a noise on the stairs, the door was unlocked and Sam's flatmates rushed in to the flat. It was only early evening, but Sam had been cautious and Audrey had been put away, hidden behind the clothes rail in his wardrobe.

'You look happy Sam, did you have a good weekend?' Sam smiled and nodded.

The flat was a hive of activity on Monday morning as they rushed around getting ready for work. Sam was up first, looking forward to it for once. The work was research in The House of Commons. An OK degree from The London School of Economics, a stint in Harvard Business School and some good family connections meant that the job interview had been a piece of cake, the result a foregone conclusion. For two years, Sam gradually grew into the job and was now regularly required to attend committees with or on behalf of his boss, a Minister who was the chairman of a group looking at the implications of Artificial Intelligence, or AI as it was called, for British business. That was how Sam had discovered the development of sexbots, from some research papers from a university in California. Not that it was mentioned to the Minister, who was supposedly a happily married family man, a fact he made plenty of use of. Having a photogenic family is a great asset in politics even in the 21st century. Over the weekend, Sam had done some excellent field work on AI but that would remain a secret. Being sexual with Audrey was stress-free after the initial learning curve, especially when compared with an embarrassing failed attempt to date Polly, a fellow student in Harvard. Just remembering it made Sam feel hot, ashamed and had inhibited any further attempts at intimacy. But that was pre-Audrey. Post-Audrey was a new ball game.

The Minister had been invited to a spring conference in California called "AI and an ageing population." Sam had been tasked to obtain the details and organise the Minister's timetable while he was at the conference. So,

Sam picked the sessions that were interesting, on carebots and gardenbots. There was no mention of sexbots. Just as well, the Minister would freak out at the very idea. He showed very little interest in the conference and Sam was unsurprised when he came in one day looking particularly serious.

'Sam, I think you will have to go to the conference on my behalf. I just have too much on at the moment. You know more about it than me, write me a report.'

'Yes of course, Minister.' *If he only knew,* thought Sam with a grin. A spring trip to California, wonderful. A post-Audrey Sam hummed a little tune.

With the excuse of getting over the jetlag, Sam made sure to arrive in Monterey a few days before the start of the conference in time for a bit of sightseeing. The aquarium was spectacular and the historical Cannery Row a reminder of Sam's favourite Steinbeck story. The town was busy. Sam thought that some people must be conference delegates. There were a few good-looking women; hopefully they were AI experts and there would be a chance to meet them. Since Audrey, things seemed to be getting better all the time. At the conference dinner table was one of these women, who was called Zoe Summers, according to the little place tag. They began a conversation.

'I'm a scientific journalist, freelance, but I'm here to get the story for a few serious newspapers. There's a lot of interest in AI at the moment, a political hot potato I believe.'

Sam smiled in agreement.

'Too true. I'm here on behalf of my boss who is a Minister.' When Zoe raised her eyebrows in surprise, Sam explained that his boss was a Government Minister. Zoe moved her chair a little closer. Sam noticed that she smelled even better than Audrey. She looked good. Not quite as perfect as Audrey but similar in some ways: slightly built with short blonde hair. When Sam had spotted her earlier in town she had been wearing running gear. She explained that running was almost an obsession, she ran before breakfast and in the late afternoon.

'I'm in training for the London marathon,' she explained. Sam was impressed; slim, fit women were a bit of a turn on.

After the conference dinner and the speeches ended, Sam and Zoe walked back to their hotel. By coincidence they were both staying at the same place just set back from the sea. They sat in the lounge and chatted a while, then Zoe said she was tired.

'See you at breakfast,' said Sam.

Back in the small room on the second floor, Sam lay on the bed and thought about Zoe. There was the same effect as usual when he thought about an attractive woman: feeling anxious, heart rate increased, slightly breathless. Better to think about Audrey, much safer, less stress.

After breakfast, Sam and Zoe walked together to the conference venue. Each day started with a plenary session. It was about the use of carebots. During the question session afterwards, Zoe put up her hand to ask a question.

'What about the effect of carebots on personal relationships?' she asked. There were no answers to the question but it initiated a lively discussion. For the rest of the day Sam and Zoe went separate ways. Sam attended a popular workshop on sexbots, which had been added to the programme at the last minute. Zoe had chosen other workshops. They bumped into each other during the lunch break.

'Fancy having dinner this evening?' asked Zoe

'Great idea, would love to.' The conference had caused a bit of a high and it seemed like a fine way to end the day.

Over dinner in an Italian themed restaurant, Zoe and Sam exchanged information about the various lectures and workshops that they had attended.

'AI is going to present significant changes for societies to get used to,' Zoe suggested.

'I agree, it will not be without problems.' Sam didn't mention that he had been to the lecture on sexbots. Zoe didn't mention it either. Sam felt uncomfortable about it. After a very pleasant meal they walked back to their hotel and sat in the lounge. They both had a whisky followed by coffee. Sam tried to get a sense of whether Zoe was interested in pursuing the evening to the next stage.

'How about having another whisky in my room?' Said with a dry mouth and thumping heart.

'Love to, shall I order us another glass?'

'No need, I've got a bottle upstairs, duty free.'

They went up to Sam's room and poured whisky into glasses from the minibar. Despite it, Sam felt the usual panic as they kissed and Zoe moved towards the bed. Zoe turned out to be a considerate, competent lover and Sam enjoyed her.

The conference finished with lunch the next day. Sam and Zoe were booked on separate flights back to the UK. Zoe had arranged to spend a few days in San Francisco visiting friends, but they agreed to meet again when she returned to London. Although Sam had enjoyed being with Zoe, as soon as it was convenient, Audrey was brought out of the wardrobe. There was something unthreatening about sessions with Audrey and Sam was able to focus on the simple physical pleasure that she enabled.

A week later, Sam received an email from Zoe.

"I'm back, would you like to come round for dinner?" So Sam went to Zoe's flat in St John's Wood. The meal was simple and delicious; a pasta dish accompanied by a bottle of Soave. Zoe clearly didn't want to spend too long on complicated cooking. They were soon in the bedroom, Sam relaxed and confident after the wine and a whisky.

Since returning from the AI conference, Sam had been working on a report for the Minister. Writing reports was easy for Sam, actually enjoyable. However, the sexbot was not mentioned in the report. Sam had mixed feelings about this omission. The lecturer at the conference had pointed out how useful sexbots could be in all sorts of situations. Sam totally agreed with these views, yet felt the need to leave the whole "sexbots" issue out of the report.

Things were developing nicely with Zoe. Sam had been introduced to some of her friends and she was looking forward to the compliment being returned. So far, Sam had found excuses and Zoe had not been invited to the flat. If the relationship was to continue to flourish it could not be postponed indefinitely. Eventually, when it was clear that Zoe was getting upset, Sam invited her to dinner. As a change from Italian food, Sam was going to prepare paella. This was the favourite meal in the flat; they all loved it and joined in the preparation so that it was a very convivial evening, especially as it was helped along with bottles of silky Rioja. All agreed that the evening was great fun and Zoe was made to feel very welcome. Sam felt the glow of being surrounded by friends and a lover. After they had loaded the dishwasher, Sam took Zoe to the bedroom. This was a new experience, a "taking your breath away" moment. As usual, Zoe behaved brilliantly. She admired the choice of colour on the walls, appreciated the collection of small black and white photographs in red frames and made compliments about the food and the company. Sam was happy and just wanted to lie on the bed curled up with Zoe and smile with delight. For once, sleep came fast and deep; it had been a busy, high-energy evening.

'What the-- oh my God!' There was a shriek and Sam was being shaken awake by Zoe. It was just daylight. Sam sat up.

'What's the matter?'

'What's this Sam?' Zoe was wearing Sam's dressing gown and holding Audrey as if she was something distasteful. In the cold light of morning, Audrey didn't look too wonderful especially next to Zoe who was pink with indignation. Sam's dressing gown of pale blue silk suited her.

'What are you doing looking in my wardrobe?' said Sam, blushing with anger mixed with embarrassment.

'Just wanted to look at your lovely clothes, I couldn't resist this dressing gown. When I took it off the rail, she just fell in front of me. Explain.'

Sam took a few deep breaths while doing some fast thinking. It was crunch time. Bluff it out or tell the truth.

'How can you have sex with this?' shouted Zoe as she threw Audrey onto the bed next to Sam.

'It's just research Zoe, calm down.'

'So what are the results of your research?'

'There's no need to be sarcastic. Very interesting as it happens.'

'For instance?'

'It's no good trying to explain when you are in this frame of mind.'

Zoe started to cry, then took off the pale blue silk dressing gown and got dressed.

'I thought we were lovers Sam, I just don't understand.'

Sam winced as she slammed the bedroom door.

There was no contact between Sam and Zoe for several days as they each tried to get their heads around what had happened. Zoe was the first to make contact. She sent Sam an email with an attachment of an article she had written about the affects of bots on personal relationships. The message said, "I'm confused Sam, please help." When Sam read the article it was clear that she was struggling. Sam phoned Zoe.

'I just want to explain that I am emotionally involved with you Zoe, not the sexbot.'

'It's objectifying and demeaning to women, Sam. How can you form any sort of bond with a machine?' asked Zoe sounding tearful.

'I've found the sexbot a great help to me, Zoe. I'm more confident and better able to look at women as people not just a sex challenge. I suppose she might seem like a threat to our relationship. She is always available, never has off days, is undemanding and didn't mind that I am female.'

'Neither do I,' said Zoe gently.

Sam smiled. Perhaps she didn't need Audrey anymore. They agreed to meet for dinner the following evening.

Sam took Audrey out of the wardrobe and laid her gently on the bed.

And yet.

The Dilemma of Owning Yourself

The TGV drew into the Gare de Lyon on time. Although it travelled at 297 kilometers an hour it had still taken over six hours from Barcelona. I expect that most of the other passengers were pleased to be arriving in Paris. The journey wasn't long enough for me. I needed more time to empty my head of the events of the summer before I could even begin to make decisions about the future. Six hours of fast travel had moved me from still, hot Barcelona to wet, windy and cold Paris. It was like moving from one season to another as the blue skies and palms were replaced by deciduous trees, bent over by the wind and lashed by the rain. It matched my mood: dark and unsettled.

My hotel was near the station, so it was quick and easy to register, leave my bags and find a restaurant. I saw it across the station square from my hotel. It was shimmering with lights and looked warm and welcoming. I was shown by a waiter to a table for two, there were no tables laid up for one. A few people glanced in my direction. I expect that they felt sorry for me, dining alone. If they only knew, I relished it. To pass the evening and to delay my thinking and deciding, I chose a four course set menu with wine. The restaurant was walled with mirrors, which reflected the lights from the rose-shaped fittings. What with the wine and the gentle background mumbles of conversation, which I didn't even try to understand, my mood lightened. For the first time in months I began to feel myself.

Looking out of the window of the restaurant, I could see people hurrying about under umbrellas. I have always liked the rain, so it was comforting after a long, hot and sometimes stormy summer.

It began early. We arrived at our villa in March. In early April the first request came from my husband's son.

"Hi Dad, what are you doing for Easter?" He has a wife and two children who come to stay with us every year. We always say that they are welcome, because they are family. Because I love my husband, David, I know that I am supposed to love his family so I make the effort. While they are with us, we have a lie-in every morning. It reduces the length of the day. The evenings are the easiest because we can hide in wine. Although the children quarrel and are naughty, we never tell them off or raise our voices. They make enough noise for all of us. I know my husband disapproves of their "spoilt behaviour" as he calls it, but we never dare challenge it. As we anxiously watch our carefully tended villa being rubbished by the visitors, my stepson says, 'Grandparents are supposed to spoil their grandchildren.' What can we say?

When they leave we are depleted, not by their absence, but by the absence of ourselves. We resolve to tackle some of the issues the next time they visit. We both know that we won't.

Their visit is closely followed by my daughter and her partner. We have to be even-handed about this. If his children can stay then so can mine, even though it means that we spend most of the summer making beds, washing towels, food shopping, tidying up, ferrying people to and from the beach and the airport: a hundred-mile round trip. It's like a job but without being paid and without weekends off.

By July it was stunningly hot. That's how I felt, stunned by the sun and the heat and brightness. So I was too feeble to resist a visit from my widowed sister and her daughter and grandson. They arrived from the airport by taxi, which must have cost a fortune.

'So good of you to have us. Hotels are so expensive in July and who wants to share a swimming pool.' I smiled: the expected response.

When my sister and family are around, David isn't. He went back to the UK for a few weeks, ostensibly to check out our boat. He doesn't get on with my niece, which I can understand. They are politically poles apart for a start and he thinks she is a racist bigot, or something along those lines. In this case, even wine can't smooth things over so the boat is a good excuse for his absence.

The one bright spot of the summer was news of my older grandson's A level results, which are excellent. So in the autumn he will be off to uni, as they call it these days. He is a lovely young man so I am pleased for him and his parents.

It's September before we have our villa to ourselves. I feel worn out and out of sorts. Over a bottle of wine before dinner, all my pent-up anger and frustration gushes out of me.

'I never want another summer like that.' I realise I'm shouting.

'You must be abnormal Janet, everyone wants to see their family, you're lucky that they want to come and see us.'

'Is it us they really want to see, or is it just a cheap holiday?' I'm still shouting. 'It's too high a price to pay.'

'What, a bit extra on the shopping and petrol bills.'

'No, it's more than that, I feel trapped. I have to say things I don't believe just to keep the peace, just because it's family.'

That night we slept in separate rooms. Over the next few days I began to recover. I went back to my reading and writing, called and met up with some friends. On the outside, life was getting back to normal. On the inside a feeling of disquiet remained.

My husband answered the phone and passed it to me. It was my grandson.

'Hi Gran, guess what, I've got a place in the uni near you. I'll be able to stay with you in the Christmas holiday.'

I managed to say, 'Congratulations.' After I hung up I started to cry. I just couldn't stop, much to my husband's annoyance. We said a lot of angry, unpleasant things to one another.

'Perhaps you need a bit of time on your own, Janet,' said my husband after I had calmed down.

'Yes I think you're right,' I heard myself whisper. My throat was too tight to speak properly.

The train journey was my idea. I thought it would give me time to get over the summer and work things out. I treated myself to a first class ticket so that I would have a big single seat and peace and quiet. The train pulled into the Gare de Lyon in the late afternoon. I still felt disturbed by the events of the summer.

The atmosphere in the restaurant, dining alone and the refreshing rain did a lot to restore my equilibrium. I knew that I had lost it over the busy summer. The next morning I felt almost light-hearted as I made my way to the Gare du Nord for my journey back to London.

It is always a pleasure to get back to our London house. I texted David to let him know of my safe arrival and saw that my grandson had left me a message.

"Hi Gran, term starting next week, can I stay for the weekend." There wasn't a question mark because it wasn't really a question in his mind. Rather a statement of intent. He knew that I wouldn't say no, because he was family. All the benefit from my train journey and dining in Paris began to seep away. So this was how it was going to be, not just in Spain but here, in London, as well.

The weekend visit wasn't too bad. Ollie, my grandson, was good company although he did talk most of the time. He suggested that we go out for Sunday lunch because he didn't want me to have to cook. We did and it cost me half my weekly food budget, at least. After he left I tried to analyse my feelings, which were decidedly mixed. Two weekends later, Ollie sent me another text asking if he could come for the weekend and bring a friend. He seemed to think that he was doing me a favour. I still didn't know how to refuse. This time he brought a girl that he had met at uni. She seemed very nice. I was relieved that there were two bathrooms in the house, because she monopolised one of them.

They were intelligent and lively young people but were only interested in me as a cook and cleaner. That is how they see me. That I had once held a senior role in a global company was of no interest to them. After each visit I felt a confusion of feelings and needed a few glasses of wine and an unburdening with a good friend to shake off the effect it had on me. I began to dread looking at my emails and texts.

David returned from Spain in the middle of November. We had been in regular contact so he knew about the visits from Ollie.

'I'm looking forward to his next one, especially if he brings a young lady. It's great to have young people around, it's good for us.' I began to see that there was no easy escape from the visits. I don't know when I made a conscious decision to act but by the end of November I had formulated a plan.

'I think I'll go and live on our boat for a couple of months,' I said casually one morning after breakfast.

'Whatever for, it's not exactly a comfortable place to be in the winter.'

'I've always had a fancy to do it. I can use the time to write.'

'Increasing 6 to gale 8, occasionally severe gale 9 later.'

I felt a sliver of fear. I could already hear the wind howling through the yacht masts. Then I calmed myself down, I wasn't going anywhere. The boat was securely tied up to the pontoon in the marina. Nevertheless, I'm not keen on severe gale 9. It will be a restless night on board. I am getting used to it, I have to. This is my home now.

Half way through the night it started to rain; it made a pattering sound on the hatch which is above my head. What with the wind whooshing in the rigging and the other bangs and slapping sounds, it was a noisy night and I was glad when daylight came.

Most of the boats have no one on board; it's December and some owners only visit when the weather is balmy. I have no idea who else is around. There is a ginger cat who has adopted me and sleeps in the cockpit at night or under the spray hood if it rains or when it fancies. I could learn a few things from that cat.

Making breakfast is a bit more challenging than in our house. For a start I have to go out in the wind and rain to turn on the gas bottle in the locker in the cockpit. Then I can make myself tea and toast. I have to admit it does taste good.

Despite the privations I am sometimes happy. My time is my own. I am beginning to remember who I am. I miss the family and feel guilty, but this is where I need to be for the time-being. Although there is not much room on the boat, it feels less claustrophobic than being with my family. On the pontoon, I am not a granny or any other kind of family member. I am the woman who lives on yacht *Silverstreak*, shared willingly with a ginger cat with a mind of his own.

Revenge Is Sweet!

'That's not allowed in the UK.' She looked up from her book. The man sitting opposite pointed at the small bowl of nuts that had been left on the table. 'Unhygienic,' he said.

'I suppose it is, I hadn't thought about it. I don't like nuts anyway.' She poured herself another glass of wine from the small jug, letting the stress of the last few days fade away.

'On holiday?' he asked.

'Afraid not. I've been at a conference in Poitiers. What about you?'

'I've been to a meeting in Le Mans, car racing.'

'Are you a racing driver?'

'Not at Le Mans. But I love driving, always have. Love cars, especially the classics. So I come over on the ferry and drive to Le Mans. I go to as many races as I can.'

Her glass was empty. It was only the smallest jug of the house wine.

'Would you like another drink? There isn't anywhere else to go around here. I can tell you that from experience.'

'Yes thank you. I'd love a glass of wine. Conferences stress me out.' He got up to fetch the drinks list from the bar. He was tall and good looking with a full head of thick silver hair. There were only a few other guests in the hotel. Although it was en route to the ferry and train shuttle it was quiet. After the noise and crowds at the conference and the long drive from Poitiers, she began to relax. He returned with the wine list and they decided on a bottle of Muscadet. For a while they had the small bar to themselves and spoke quietly so that it seemed intimate.

He told her that his name was Malcolm and that he worked in IT. He asked about the conference and joked when she explained that she was a psychologist: 'Does that mean you'll be analyzing me?'

She smiled. *He might be attractive, but he's not original.*

Compared with the serious colleagues at the conference, Malcolm seemed light and amusing. He told her about the thrills and drama of motor racing and she laughed at the jokes he made, mainly about himself and his motoring disasters. He didn't ask her name and she didn't offer it, relishing her anonymity.

'So what car do you drive, Malcolm?'

'My pride and joy is my Jaguar E-Type.'

'That's one of my favourite cars ever. Lucky you. What colour is it?'

'British racing green. It's too dark to see it now, I'll show you in the morning.'

They finished the bottle of wine and moved into the dining room. On her way back from a visit to the cloakroom she stepped outside to look at his car. There was an E-Type in the car park. She could see it clearly from the lights of the hotel. But it wasn't British racing green. It was pillar box red. *Strange*, she thought. *Is he colour blind or a liar?*

After a surprisingly good meal and a jug of the house red wine, a large one this time, they returned to the cozy bar. The few other guests had gone to their rooms so they had it to themselves again. Malcolm got them both a brandy. He had a fund of anecdotes and jokes so they had lots of laughs. By midnight the alcohol had worked its magic and she was struggling to keep her eyes open.

'I'm really tired.' Her voice sounded funny, even to her. She stood up and nearly fell over.

'Here, take my arm,' said Malcolm, 'I'll walk you to your room.'

When she woke up, she knew that something had happened. The bed linen made it clear, if there had been any doubt. She had a vague recollection of being with a man. It wasn't a dream, it was real.

Oh my God, this can't have happened to me. How can I have been so stupid?

She eased herself out of the tangle of crumpled bedclothes and looked out of the window. Although it was still early, there was no red E-Type in the car park.

Why am I not surprised.

She checked the time. It was still possible to get the shuttle if she got a move on. It would mean missing breakfast, but she had never felt less like eating, so that was no problem. When she was checking out, she thought that the young French man on the desk gave her a funny look. Her face felt hot and a headache was developing but she smiled and made all the usual polite responses. The day suited her mood: grey and depressing. The drive was straightforward and she arrived in time to make her booked train and get a cup of coffee. She drove her car up the ramp and into the train with a sense of relief. While waiting for the journey to begin she sipped her coffee. When the train left the station, in the privacy of her car, she wept. After a quarter of an hour she realised that she couldn't cry and think. So she stopped crying.

By the time that the train emerged from the tunnel at the end of the crossing, she had made a decision.

I will make sure that he is called to account.

There were matters to attend to resulting from the conference, as well as her regular academic work, so she was busy. But there were some quiet moments. During one of the quiet times she arranged to have her hair cut in a short, modern style and, to cheer herself up, splashed out on blonde highlights. She lost a bit of weight, not by dieting, but because some days she couldn't be bothered to eat. When she thought about what had happened, her memory of the last part of the evening was confused. She knew that she had drunk rather a lot of wine. Normally a good sleeper, she now often had restless nights.

Was it my own fault? Did I encourage him, how much am I culpable?

She went over the events, time and time again, trying to be clear in her own mind. Because of her uncertainty, she told no-one, not even her best friend. There was so much going on in the world about sexual abuse of women that she found it hard to forget about it. Some of her friends noticed that she was "in a funny place", as they put it. She told them that she was finding her work hard going. As the weeks passed, she thought about it less often. When she did allow herself to try and remember what had happened, she felt guilty.

In early September, she was invited by a colleague, John, to a motoring event, The Goodwood Revival. He explained that it was the epitome of classic car racing. Since she was free that weekend, she accepted. He explained that staff would be dressed in period outfits and visitors were encouraged to do the same. She looked on-line at previous Revival meetings. There were plenty of ideas to inspire her. She enjoyed dressing up. In consultation with John, they agreed to dress in car mechanics overalls. On Saturday morning at the crack of dawn, he picked her up and they drove to the Goodwood Revival venue, arriving by eight o'clock. The weather was glorious, blue clear skies, a gentle breeze, perfect for racing. The car park was already filling up with a variety of cars, many of them old but in beautiful condition, lovingly maintained by their proud owners.

Since they had left so early, on arrival they had breakfast at one of the many restaurants. After that they wandered around the Revival paddocks where the drivers and mechanics were putting the final touches to their cars and showing them off to the classic car fans who were Goodwood Revival members and had paddock passes. There was a range of old cars from a 1958 Austin 35 to 1960's Formula One racing cars.

When she saw him, her heart started to race and she held onto John.

'Are you alright? You look a bit pale.'

'Just feeling a bit giddy, too much sun, I'll put my sunglasses on.' She took her sunglasses and a peaked cap from her rucksack. He wouldn't recognise her now.

He probably won't even remember me.

He was standing next to an E-type. In the sun she could see his reflection in the shiny red paintwork. She noted the race number on the bonnet and side of the car.

'I still feel a bit shaky, John. Do you mind if we go and have a coffee. We can come back later.'

'Of course, I could do with a sit down.' They left the paddock and went to the members' enclosure.

'Shall we look at the Race Card and decide which we want to watch? There's so much else to see, we need to make plans. I would like to see the Mini Coopers and the E-Types race. What do you fancy?'

'I'm a Porsche and McLaren man myself, so we may need to split up and get together later for a drink and dinner. Is that OK with you?'

She studied the Race Card. The E-Type and number that she had noted on his car enabled her to identify him. The driver was called Malcolm.

What a surprise, I expected that to be a lie.

She now knew his surname, Bartley-Grant. He was racing on Sunday afternoon. That meant she had twenty-four hours.

'See you later, John. Enjoy your afternoon and, by the way, thank you for inviting me.' He sauntered off and she got up and went to the cloakroom to check on her appearance. With a scarf around her hair under the peaked cap, sunglasses and bright red lipstick, even her own mother would be hard put to recognise her.

I look pretty good in this get up. I'll pull the belt in a notch. It's funny how men's clothes can be so flattering and empowering.

Although it was lunch time, food was out of the question due to the butterflies in her stomach. She felt focused. It gave her energy, made her eyes shine and delivered a flattering colour to her complexion. She walked back to the paddock. Malcolm was still fine-tuning his car. He looked dashing in dark blue overalls and a red cravat, which showed up to perfection his head of silver hair. The car was being admired by two young women, both dressed in mini-skirts and long white boots. She could hear them laughing at his self-deprecating jokes. Even the thought of the racing didn't seem to dampen his chatting-up talents.

Eventually they moved away. So she approached the car and took out her phone.

'Beautiful! Is it OK if I take a picture? For my brother, he just loves these cars.'

I'm banking on him being vain enough to agree.

'If you could just stand there. Your blue overalls look so good next to the red car.'

Of course, he did. He loved it, a big smile on his handsome face. I almost believed that he would get out a mirror and check his hair was in place.

He showed no sign of remembering her and asked to see the photograph.

'That's good, well done.' He looked at his watch. 'It's lunch time, why don't you join me? I'm Malcolm, by the way.'

I may not be able to force any food down, but this is too good to miss.

'OK, thanks. I hadn't noticed that it was time for lunch.' He led the way to the Drivers' Club.

'What would you like to drink?' he asked.

I'm not making that mistake again.

'Just a sparkling water please, I'm not too good with alcohol at lunch time.'

'Me neither, I like to save it for the evening,' he said with a grin. 'You might as well tell me your name.'

'Sarah.'

To her surprise, when she looked at the menu, she realised that she was hungry and actually fancied a Caesar salad. They ordered their food and he began to tell her stories about motor racing. She had heard one or two of them before, from him. She said nothing and laughed and smiled when necessary.

He's so easy to be with, as charming as they come.

'I assume that you are racing this weekend?'

'Yes, tomorrow. Hope the weather stays like this. But it probably won't, there's rain forecast.'

'Does that matter?'

'Not half, tearing around in the wet isn't my idea of fun. All the spray ruins the visibility.'

'It sounds dangerous.'

'It is.' He went quiet as he seemed to be contemplating tomorrow's race. She looked at his face, which seemed sharpened by anxiety and, to her amazement, she felt a wave of pity for him.

'I think I need to get back,' he said. 'I'm expecting Jim, my racing partner.' He paid for lunch and they walked slowly back to the paddock. The sun was shining and it was hard to believe the weather forecast. At the red E-Type, a young man in overalls was looking under the bonnet. He looked as if he knew what he was doing.

'Hi Jim, great to see you. Is she looking alright?'

'Fantastic mate, the money was well spent.'

'Glad to hear it, but time will tell.' He drew Sarah aside. 'I know we've just met, but do you think you can do me a favour?' He ran his hand through his hair. Before she could reply he carried on, 'I get nervous the evening before a race. I can't bear to be on my own. Do you think you could have dinner with me?'

This is an opportunity, not a threat.

'What about your racing partner?'

'It doesn't work being with Jim. He wants to talk about racing tactics and winds me up even more. Please, I would really appreciate it. Dinner would be on me, of course.'

'I'll have to make a phone call to see if I can change an existing arrangement.'

'Understood.'

'I'll do it now.'

She walked away from Malcolm so that he couldn't overhear her conversation. She lied to her colleague, saying that she had bumped into an old friend from university.

'OK Malcolm, what are the arrangements?'

'If we meet here at six, would that suit you?'

What have I let myself in for? I don't have anything to wear.

'Fine, I assume overalls aren't the dress code for the evening?'

'No, I'm going to take you to somewhere special.'

'Can we go in the E-Type?'

'Sure, I'll see you at six.' They smiled at each other and Sarah left the paddock, waving goodbye to Jim. She looked at her watch. Three o'clock. Time to do some clothes shopping.

There was no shortage of shops, many selling vintage clothes, from cocktail dresses to military inspired uniforms. A simple black dress would do the job and would be suitable for a pub or a smart restaurant. She avoided low necks and short skirts and chose a well-cut severe style in silk crepe. To enliven the outfit she bought handmade silver earrings and matching bracelet, and a pair of Louboutin shoes with red soles. The whole outfit set her back by almost a month's salary.

I don't have a plan. I'll go with the flow and find my chance.

There was plenty of time to collect sugar sachets from the many coffee shops. She knew that sugar in the petrol tank would stop the car running so that he couldn't win his race. She wasn't sure how much was required so she collected enough to fill two mugs. That would have to do. She still had time to find a suitable cloakroom and get herself dressed for the evening. Her overalls were disposed of in a rubbish bin. Since she had told John that she would make her own way home, they were no longer required.

When she emerged from the cloakroom, she noticed that several men looked at her for a little longer than she was used to.

That month's salary was well spent.

The sugar was heavy in her handbag and it seemed a long walk back to the paddock in the high heels. She hadn't thrown her sensible shoes away, they might be needed. They were adding to the weight in her handbag. Malcolm, dressed in a light suit, was waiting for her. A blue open neck shirt did wonders for his silver hair and blue eyes.

He's a very attractive man, no doubt about it.

'Hello again, you look great. I really love that dress.' He touched her shoulder. 'I'm looking forward to dinner. I've booked us into a restaurant. It's a few miles away; every restaurant in a ten-mile radius was already full.'

'So I'll get a longer ride in the E-Type.'

He smiled, took her arm and led her away from his car and out of the paddock.

'Oh, I thought we were going in your car?'

'We are, but not this one. It's all ready for the race tomorrow so it stays here.'

They walked for some time towards the car park.

'I hope we aren't going much further, these shoes are for riding in cars not walking'

'Here we are,' he said and opened the door of an E-Type. It was British racing green.

'How many cars have you got, Malcolm?'

'Only two E-Types, this and the red racing one.

I'm confused.

She got into the car as elegantly as possible. He closed her door and slipped into the driving seat. As she settled herself and put on the seat belt, he turned to her.

'Thank you so much for this Sarah, I feel myself relaxing already.'

Being in the handsome, powerful car driven by an expert, a racing driver no less, was a new experience for her. When they stopped at traffic lights she noticed that the car attracted attention.

I shouldn't really be enjoying this. It's supposed to be about getting my own back.

They slowed down as Malcolm drove through enormous wrought iron gates, down a gravel drive to a country hotel.

'Are we here already?' she asked.

He parked the car in the residents' car park.

'Are you staying here?'

'Yes, that's how I was able to book a table for dinner.'

They entered the hotel foyer and he took her arm and ushered her into the bar for a pre-dinner drink. She was pleased to have a sit down in a comfortable armchair looking out over a pretty, formal garden. It had been a strange and tiring day. He ordered two glasses of champagne.

I'm on my guard this time.

They were brought the menus.

'You remind me of someone. Have we met before somewhere?'

'No, we haven't.'

'Would you like another drink?'

She smiled and refused.

'I don't think I will either. I want a clear head for the race tomorrow. It's not until the afternoon but Jim and I have work to do. We want to do well this year.'

Her look was a question.

'We had to withdraw last year after two laps. Don't want that to happen again.'

They moved into the restaurant. It was cool and still light. Malcolm chose a bottle of white Burgundy.

'I think you'll like this. This will be it for tonight, if that's alright with you?'

Sarah was surprised that she had mixed feelings about the suggestion, but she agreed. By the time they had come to the end of dinner, the sky was beginning to darken. At Malcolm's suggestion they took their coffee in the hotel lounge. They sat in comfortable armchairs in the candlelit room and continued to talk as if they had been friends for ever. Sarah wished that she could cut their last meeting out of her life story.

'I suppose I should be thinking about getting home.'

'Why don't you stay here? My room is huge, there's a sofa bed.'

'Thank you. If you're sure?'

'I hope you don't snore, I need a good night's sleep tonight. Tomorrow is a big day.'

He stood up and walked towards the lift to the hotel rooms. She followed. He hadn't exaggerated, his room was spacious and there was a sofa bed.

Why do I feel disappointed, rather than relieved?

'It's too early to go to bed, I wouldn't be able to sleep. Shall I make us a drink, non-alcoholic of course?'

'OK, can I have coffee please?'

She sat in one of a pair of armchairs set either side of a long window looking out over gardens. He put a cup of coffee on a small table and sat in the armchair facing her.

'I can't thank you enough for this evening, Sarah. Last year was a missed opportunity, which I don't want to repeat. I've had enough of those already this year.'

'You mean the race?'

'Not just that.' She stayed silent. 'I met a woman in a hotel on my way back from Le Mans. You remind me of her, same eyes, similar build. We had dinner together, we just clicked somehow.'

'What happened?' she asked and held her breath, waiting for his answer.

'She seemed as keen as I was. She was lovely, I couldn't believe my luck. She drank a lot of wine. Well I did too, but it seemed to affect her more than me. By the end of the evening she was a bit drunk, needed help to get to her room.'

'So you went to her room?'

'Yes, when we got there she invited me to bed, the alcohol didn't affect her as far as that was concerned. It was lovely.' His face softened at the recollection.

'So how was it a missed opportunity?'

'I had an early ferry the next morning. So I had to leave very early. She was out like a log so I just slipped away. I left a note with my number on it on the bedside table, but I haven't heard from her.' He spoke in a low voice, a sad voice.

Sarah desperately wanted a sip of coffee, her throat was dry. She moved to pick up the cup but her hand shook, so she put it down again. She felt a need for the truth. It came flooding over her. She felt heat in her face and a wash of shame as she acknowledged to herself that she had used alcohol to give up control of her behaviour.

'Are you alright, I hope I haven't upset you?' He got up from his chair and sat on the floor next to her.

'Yes, I'm alright. Thank you for telling me that.'

'I don't know why I did. I just feel that I can talk to you. You're not crying are you?'

'No. Well, yes I am a bit upset. I'll tell you about it some time. But I think we should go to bed now, you want to be at your best for the race tomorrow. If you pass me my bag, I'll use the bathroom.'

He picked up her handbag.

'Whatever are you carrying, it weighs a ton?'

'Sugar sachets, I collect them. I think I overdid it. I can't be bothered to take them home. Is there a rubbish bin here?' He pointed to a small bin next to the desk. She stood up, took the bag of sugar sachets and emptied them into the bin.

The Flying Club

The pine needles pricked her bare back despite the blanket. Julia soon forgot them as Ian began kissing her eyelids, her mouth, her throat, then moving down to latch on to her breasts. Even though they were in the shade of the pine trees, it was hot and silent.

For the rest of her life the smell of pine trees would bring back memories of the all-consuming sex, overshadowed by deep, black sadness.

The affair, if you could call it that, had started six weeks ago. They had known one another for a while since meeting at the Flying Club where her husband, James, flew his Hawker Hurricane. Not the real thing but a model. The club members met twice a week to fly – with considerable skill – aeroplanes of all kinds. They were all kinds of men. In a past life some of them had flown real planes. Men united by the thrill of seeing their model planes soar and dip in the clear, turquoise Spanish sky and the relief when they landed, still in one piece, on the dry grass. Because they were made of fragile balsawood, flying was best done in light airs; often the calm morning before the afternoon winds. The only women around were wives and friends who came to watch and serve the morning coffee.

The flying field was surrounded by orange groves and rows of almond trees. In the distance the jagged shapes of the mountains made a dark backdrop. Julia was enchanted by the whole experience. When the model planes were in the sky they became real, beautiful. They flew fast and spoke to her of freedom. She stood at the high safety fencing to watch her husband take his turn to fly his Hawker Hurricane.

'Beautiful isn't it? He's a good flyer.'

Julia turned around to respond to Ian, who had come to stand next to her.

'I love it,' replied Julia with a smile.

'Why don't you have a go?'

'Fly James' plane. You must be joking, he won't let me touch it, let alone fly it. It's his pride and joy.'

'But would you like to?'

Julia nodded.

'I'll give you a go some time with one of my planes.'

Julia was surprised and flattered by his attention. Ian was the club's ace flyer, regularly winning international competitions. Until recently he had been an airline captain and still flew the real thing from time to time. The few women who came to watch were mostly ignored by the men, who were more intent on getting their planes ready for flying. They grouped around the tables available for this task. Ian moved away from Julia to the table to get his plane ready. Club members usually stopped what they were doing to watch him fly his Spitfire. They were not disappointed. The Spitfire was beautiful, gleaming silver with a red nose, a white propeller and the RAF red, white and blue roundel on the side. As if that wasn't enough colour, the wings were black and white stripes. Julia watched, like the rest of the club. As the Spitfire rose and fell, she felt a fluttering of anticipation and held on to the safety fence as if her legs were going to give way.

Gradually, as the flyers had all had their turn, people drifted away to pack the planes into their vehicles. James, on a high after a successful morning, suggested that they drive to a beach restaurant for lunch.

'Everything alright Julia, you're a bit quiet?'

On Tuesday mornings, Julia attended a Spanish class in the local town. Although only making slow progress, she was determined to learn the language of the country she was beginning to know and enjoy. Usually, after the class had finished, a few of them went to a nearby bar for a coffee. Sitting at a table inside the bar was Ian. She smiled and gave him a little wave of her hand as she ordered her *café con leche*. As her companions got up to leave, he came up to her. '*Hola* Julia. Can I get you another coffee?'

She made the fateful decision to accept. That was how it began.

She stopped going to the class and instead spent Tuesday mornings and sometimes the afternoon with Ian. They drove independently to a "Parc Natural" on the coast where they would walk past the picnic tables, deep into the pine forest. Ian brought a blanket and a bottle of wine and they spent the time discovering that they enjoyed the same sexual pleasures. Afterwards they would walk back to their parked cars. Julia often felt too lightheaded to drive and just sat in her car until she felt recovered enough to drive home.

One or two of her female friends commented on how well she was looking. She could see for herself in the mirror that the affair was making her beautiful. James, her husband, didn't appear to notice. He was totally occupied with organising the summer party for the Flying Club. She was used to being invisible as far as he was concerned so she wasn't really surprised.

Julia lived for her Tuesdays with Ian. She knew hardly anything about him and he showed no interest in her other than exploring her body and finding out how to give her the most pleasure. It was as if they lived in a bubble separate from the rest of the world. Some days it seemed too hot to lie together but, despite that, they discovered that their moist coupling created an intimacy which neither had previously experienced.

The morning of the summer party was perfect for flying. It was hot with a cloudless sky and very little wind. James and Julia arrived early at the field to set out some chairs under the tin roof for the spectators. Several cold boxes contained food and drink, and Julia had packed a large crate full of picnic plates, glasses and utensils. The members started to arrive and the flyers began to set up their planes on the tables to prepare them for flight. There was a party buzz. Julia was aware of Ian at a table working on his Spitfire. Her husband was working on his plane at the adjacent table. They chatted together and pored over each other's planes, discussing trims, checks and other details fascinating to enthusiastic fliers. Julia set out the glasses and chatted with other wives and friends about what time to light the BBQ.

James indicated that he was ready to fly. He strolled into the flying field, placed the airplane on the ground and started the engine. With the control box in both hands, he nodded at the spectators as his plane soared into the sky. His was not the only one, another was already in flight and the two handlers skillfully kept them away from one another so that they whooshed and circled like big birds. After five minutes, James landed his plane to a round of applause. He left the field smiling with relief.

Julia noticed that Ian was no longer at his table, he was talking and working with some people at other tables and gradually weaved his way towards her. She was arranging cutlery when he came up and stood very close behind her. She could feel his heat and her own. They made desultory small talk while all the time she was aware of his effect on her; her heart rate increased, her face flushed, she felt breathless. In the sky, planes were soaring and diving so that she felt giddy. He gently touched the small of her back and she inhaled his familiar smell. Then he was gone, walking purposefully to his table and plane. He picked it up and walked towards the flying field, which was enclosed by high safety fencing. Some people stopped what they were doing to watch, they knew that he flew fast and clean, so there was an air of expectancy as the plane took off and climbed high. The watchers were confident in his skills so they could just relax and enjoy the spectacle. He made the plane fly upside down, turn sharp circles so that there were small gasps of surprise and delight. The speed increased, Julia had been told that the planes can travel at seventy miles an hour. After ten minutes of spectacular flying, Julia, who was watching Ian, not the plane, saw a look of panic cross his face.

The Spitfire was out of control. Ian worked the control box but the plane was not responding. It dived at great speed towards a group of people who had just arrived and were unloading their car. They were on the right side of the safety fence but the plane seemed to be programmed to make them its target. It missed the car and crashed into a child.

Suddenly there was screaming, shouting and crying.

Ian looked at the control unit, unable to believe what had happened. Then he cried out.

'Oh my God, what the hell…' He started to sweat as he staggered towards the gate, out of the flying field. Distracted by Julia, for the first time ever, he had not carried out his final check before flying. Julia was overcome with hysterical sobbing and sank to her knees. James came over to help her up and put his arms around her. The ambulance sirens could be heard in the distance.

For several weeks, Julia avoided both the flying club and the Spanish class. She sat at home looking out of the window at the sea. Sometimes she tried to distract her thoughts by reading but usually, after an unsuccessful attempt, she put the book aside. An investigation was being held to find out how such a dreadful accident could have happened. One of the other wives told her that Ian had returned to England and that his Spanish villa was up for sale.

At the start of the autumn term, Julia returned to the Spanish class. She looked pale, unlike her usual suntanned self.

'Welcome back Julia, it's good to see you again,' said the teacher. 'We missed you.'

Julia found the class hard going, she had forgotten so much during her absence. It seemed a long time until the coffee break. Over coffee, other students talked about their summer. Julia said nothing.

'It was nice to meet your husband, Julia,' said the teacher. 'How is he getting on with that flying club?'

'I didn't know you had met James. When was that?'

'Didn't he say? He came to look for you a couple of times. They were the times you missed the class.'

'Oh right, of course, now you mention it,' said Julia.

During the second half of the class, Julia found it hard to concentrate on the lesson. An image flashed into her head. She realised that it had been there since the awful day in the flying field. It made her catch her breath. But it was crystal clear. It was of her husband leaning over a table and working on a plane, alone. Not his plane, but Ian's Spitfire.

The Living in
La-La Land Mission

It was raining on the day I collected my award from the palace. Of course my parents were delighted and insisted on taking me out to lunch after the ceremony. They couldn't tell whether my wet face was due to the rain or my tears. I worked hard to appear OK, but my face ached from wanting to have a good cry. Eventually, just when I was thinking it would never end, my mother stood up.

'We need to go. We can just make the next train if we hurry. Thank you, Elaine, dear for inviting us, we are very proud of you.'

I dragged myself back to my flat in Putney, poured myself a glass of wine and let the tears come.

My parents had been so pleased when I got the job at the Treasury. They were more delighted than me. I don't have a husband and children so they have to find something to say when they meet up with their friends. "Aim for the stars" is our family motto. They have always had high expectations and I don't want to be a disappointment. They are always going on about my sister who is a successful lawyer, so I have to offer them something.

Of course I find my job interesting. Who wouldn't! The Treasury has mighty tentacles and the decisions we make have serious implications. To be honest, I think some of my colleagues are power freaks.

About nine months ago, my boss asked me to go to a conference in Munich on a mission, as he put it, to find out about the economic theories being proposed by a Professor Adam Winter.

'He's a dangerous man, Elaine. He could undermine all our work.'

Well I could hardly refuse. In my job, I go to a lot of conferences. I usually enjoy them. I'm not much good at the socialising but I like the intellectual stimulation. The conference was attended by a mix of European economists from the academic and financial worlds. There were a few special advisers and members of think tanks, the usual sort of crowd. I studied the programme and noted every session that involved Professor Winter. I went to all of them. He was an attractive man, in his late fifties, confident and charming. The lecture I needed to hear was about economic growth. It was well attended.

'Growth is like God,' he said. 'Believe in it and all will be well. But it is a false God. It cannot go on forever and we need to find ways of living in its absence. We can't go on living in la-la land.'

I was somewhat surprised at his view. I'm something of an economist myself and I know that government borrowing relies on the premise of continual economic growth. If Professor Adam Winter could undermine that premise, then my boss was right. He is a dangerous man. Perhaps that added to his attractiveness. I thought he was gorgeous. He was tall, slim and elegant with short grey hair. He fizzed with energy and engaged with the other participants in a friendly sort of way. I didn't like his economic theories but I liked him. After his lecture he took questions. The audience couldn't seem to get enough of his views.

'Even if we agreed with you, how can we get the public to accept the idea of no growth?' I asked.

'Good question.' He smiled at me. 'It won't be easy but it can be done, we need to change what we value and have less love of money and material possessions.'

At the end of the session, I stayed behind to ask Professor Winter some more questions. When there was just the two of us left, he explained that he had to leave for another meeting.

'Perhaps we could continue our discussion over a glass of wine later.'

Of course I accepted. I am on a mission. Back in my hotel I phoned my boss.

'You are right about Professor Winter. His ideas would be a threat to the status quo. We are meeting for a drink this evening so I will see what else I can find out.'

I made a bit of an effort to look good for my meeting with Professor Winter. I felt as if I were dressing for something important, like an interview. I even got butterflies in my stomach. We had agreed to meet at a wine bar near to the conference centre and when I arrived, he was already there talking with a few young colleagues who sat around him as if he were their guru. He looked smart so I was glad that I was wearing my most attractive dress. Although I say so myself, black suits me. He looked at the low neckline with a smile.

'What would you like to drink? Please, call me Adam.'

'My name is Elaine and I'd like a glass of white wine please.'

By the way he smiled at me I knew that I had made a hit. I had forgotten how powerful that feeling of sexual connection can be. The eye contact, the basic recognition that one human being grants to another. It even affects my breathing; I feel as if there isn't enough air. I hadn't felt it for a long time and I realised that I missed it. He answered questions from colleagues and I could see that he was passionate about his economic theories. Gradually they drifted away in ones and twos. Eventually we were alone as the others had gone off to the conference disco. We moved closer together. He was a dangerous man without a doubt. I knew that I needed to be careful.

'Have you got to get back to London when the conference finishes?'

'Not immediately,' I answered.

'I have some colleagues at the university in Freiberg who have invited me for a few days to give a seminar. Ever been to Freiberg?'

'No.'

'It's a beautiful old town; how about joining me for a few days?'

I was a bit surprised to say the least but tried not to show it. Of course I accepted the invitation. I had that feeling of overstepping the mark but I told myself that this would help me with my mission. I am very good at finding excuses for my actions.

The last day of the conference dragged because I already wanted to be somewhere else. We had arranged to meet at the station to get the train to Freiberg. I was aware that nobody knew where I was going, not even my boss. I liked that idea. It gave me a sense of freedom and that I was embarking on an adventure. I could certainly do with a bit of excitement. During the journey we talked about his lecture. He didn't ask me about my work. I wasn't surprised, most people don't.

When we arrived in Freiberg, Adam suggested that I have lunch by myself while he went to the university to meet up with his colleagues. As soon as Adam had left, I made a phone call before settling down to my meal. I felt a little nervous at the thought of meeting up with his contacts. At about four o'clock, Adam joined me and outlined his plan. I agreed, trying not to sound too eager. We would spend the night together and join his friends the next day. He had already booked us in to a hotel. We dined in the hotel restaurant. I took my time over the meal. The wine was good so I drank more than I usually do.

'Are you OK?' asked Adam.

'Fine, it's just that I'm not used to this sort of thing.'

I had a sense that it was not unusual behaviour for Adam. Eventually I felt that I would just look silly if I delayed any longer.

'Shall we have coffee in our room?' I said, surprising myself. He really was very attractive. When we got to the room, Adam dimmed the lights and poured two glasses of wine. He gently removed my clothes, stroked my hair and whispered compliments. I haven't had a lot of experience but I felt it was all fine. He took of his clothes and cuddled me until I felt relaxed. I had never enjoyed sex so much before. There was a lot of kissing and cuddling and I forgot all about economics. Later I couldn't get to sleep. I reminded myself that this was not about forming a relationship with this lovely man. I was here to do a job.

Adam's colleagues had invited us to stay with them in their summer house, which was situated outside the city in the mountains. Early the next morning we were picked up by car and driven to the house. It was small and cosy, looking out over the valley and made largely of wood. I felt uncomfortable at first being with Gerhard and his wife, Gisela. They were clearly pleased to be with Adam again and behaved as if they were old friends. We had breakfast together, then Adam and Gerhard drove off to the university leaving me to spend the day with his wife. It wasn't really what I had expected when I accepted the invitation but I decided to make the best of it. I had a job to do after all.

'Have you known Adam long?' I asked Gisela.

'Yes, we know him and his family very well. Gerhard and Adam have worked together before and they meet regularly at conferences. We have spent time with him and his family in London.'

I changed the subject. I didn't want to know any more at the moment. When the two men got back at the end of their working day, they continued their discussions about economic growth and I could see that their ideas were very different from the line our government and especially the chancellor were following. They discussed the danger of believing that growth was here to stay. In their view, since resources were finite, growth was too. I just listened, asked a few questions and kept my views to myself. However, I had to admit that they had presented some very convincing arguments. I knew from my work that the growth figures weren't what they seemed and were usually talked up. I was beginning to think that they had a point, which my boss was going to find hard to swallow.

After supper, Adam suggested that we go to bed. I expected that our hosts would look uncomfortable.

'Would it be alright if we joined you?' asked Gerhard. 'It's been a while since we were together.'

Adam looked at me.

'Is it OK with you?' he asked.

I was too shocked to think clearly. Nobody made eye contact with me. *I'm out of my comfort zone and it's good for me,* I told myself.

So I nodded, 'Yes, fine,' and hoped they wouldn't notice that I was blushing.

For the next couple of hours we all enjoyed each other in as many ways that they could think of. It was all new to me. We changed partners and took it in turns to watch. Eventually, Adam and Gerhard pleasured each other encouraged by Gisela.

'Are you alright, Elaine?' asked Adam.

I was surprised by how much I enjoyed myself. Everyone was gentle and considerate and I have to say that my embarrassment soon faded. I found it all very exciting. We drank plenty of wine. At about 2 a.m., Adam and Gerhard left to go to the other bedroom and I fell asleep with Gisela. When I woke up the next morning, Adam was asleep next to me. It seemed as if I had imagined the whole thing.

We got up slightly later than on the previous day. At breakfast, no-one said anything about the sexual adventures the previous night and Adam and Gerhard went off for their day's work at the university. After they had left, Gisela offered to drive me into Freiberg so that I could do some shopping since she had her own plans for the day. I did some desultory shopping and then phoned my boss. We had a long discussion. Afterwards I found a cafe where I could get a glass of wine. I needed time to think about what he had asked me to do.

That evening we were all together again for dinner. Afterwards I said that I had enjoyed the sexual pleasures the previous evening. I felt very embarrassed saying it, although it was true.

'Let's have another lovely time,' said Gerhard.

This time I joined in with even more enthusiasm, although I didn't drink much, only enough so that I was part of the group. I poured large glasses of wine for the others. My mobile phone, fully charged, was in my handbag, which I discretely took into the bedroom. Once again after several hours of sexual games, Adam and Gerhard moved into the other bedroom. I snuggled down in bed with Gisela. When I could tell from her regular breathing that she was asleep, I got up quietly and opened the door of the other bedroom. The bedside lamp was on and I could see that Adam and Gerhard were wrapped around each other. The bed was dishevelled and they were both naked. I took several photographs then went quietly back to bed, my mobile phone safe in my handbag. When I woke up in the morning, Adam was sleeping next to me.

The next day, Gisela drove us to the station and we caught the train to Munich. We had planned to spend a night there before flying back to the UK. So we booked into a hotel, had dinner in the restaurant then went to bed. I didn't need to linger over the meal this time. Adam had an early flight to Heathrow and I had a later one to Gatwick. We didn't talk about our time with Gerhard and Gisela. Adam didn't say anything about meeting up again when we were back in London. I knew why. Although Adam hadn't mentioned it, my boss had told me all about him. He had two children and a wife who worked as a researcher in his department in the university. Nevertheless, I hoped that we would meet again. Adam left for the airport after an early breakfast. We kissed each other goodbye.

'See you sometime,' I said. 'Thank you for a great time. Much more interesting than sightseeing in Munich.' Talk about an understatement.

It was a wrench seeing him go. I was shocked how soon I had formed a strong attachment to him. He seemed a special person to me. Yet I knew that I was being asked to help to destroy him, certainly to put a spanner in the works regarding his career. I could still change my mind. If I did I would fail in my mission.

I couldn't stop thinking about it all when I was on the plane coming home, it seemed unreal. Yet I had never felt more excited and alive. I had done the task I had been set and I felt important. Of course I knew that I couldn't tell anybody but I felt good anyway. I suppose this is what power feels like. I began to understand my power freak colleagues. The sex was lovely but the feeling of power was even better. As instructed by my boss I emailed the photographs of Adam and Gerhardt to his personal computer.

'Well done Elaine, I knew I could rely on you,' was his response.

* * *

Since I've been back at work, I must say that I've thought about Adam and his economic theories. He was probably right; growth can't go on forever. I've heard nothing more about my mission. Perhaps they didn't need to use the photographs. I hope so because he was a good man. In different circumstances, maybe we could have developed our relationship. I've thought of trying to contact him, in fact I phoned his department at the university. They said that he was on leave. I even emailed him but he didn't reply. I think that the sex was good because I liked him so much. I even respect his ideas. I've started to read his papers on economic growth. Interesting!

Obviously working in the Treasury we are all interested in the budget. We have a lot of work to do before and after. It's a very exciting time. The chancellor has been working on his budget speech for months. He keeps the details a secret, even from most of his staff, including me of course. I watched him deliver it on the TV in the office. It's an important day for us all.

'We have been through a difficult time,' he said in a grave voice. 'However, the economy is growing, albeit slowly, but with our projected growth over the next few months we will be able to get back on track.'

I knew what that meant, more borrowing. I had a sinking feeling in my stomach and I knew that I had been kidding myself. The photographs had been used to silence Adam and now there was no-one to disagree. The mission to go on living in la-la land had been a success.

Twice as Much Husband and Half as Much Money

'Twice as much husband and half as much money.'

'Doesn't bear thinking about,' said Pat as she got up to get another cup of coffee. The other women in the group smiled. Although we had only met the previous day, we had already had a few interesting chats. The atmosphere at the course encouraged frank discussions, helped no doubt, by the generous glasses of wine at lunch.

When my husband, Paul, invited me to go on the company-sponsored pre-retirement course, I jumped at the chance because it meant a few days in a five star hotel near the sea. I now know quite a lot about pensions and how to look after my health as I age. According to the course tutors, when there is a big change in life, like retirement, it can cause problems. It makes sense when you think about it. I'm not worried about the money. Paul had a very well paid job and has a fabulous pension. It's the twice as much husband that concerns me. It will be more than that in my case. He's spent a lot of time in the USA at the company headquarters so in the last couple of years we've hardly spent any time together. There was a rather worrying session about how many hours people spend at work and the problems that can arise when they have all that extra time to fill.

'Go round the world,' suggested Pat. 'See all the places you've always wanted to visit but never had the time.'

'I like the sound of that, let's get away from the winter weather. What do you think?' my husband asked.

To cut a long story short, that's what we did. When I woke up in the mornings, it took me a few minutes to work out where I was. Five star international hotels are rather similar wherever they are. I enjoyed waking up to a turquoise sky and got used to knowing the intensity of the sun by the blackness of the shadow made by the window frames. It was lovely to awaken to the smell of almond blossom, the slap of water against a wall, the braying of a donkey, the eye-stinging effect of farmers' early morning fires, the eerie sound of the muezzin, the smell of strong coffee and fresh oranges, the soothing motion of a boat. There were vibrant colours to enjoy, spicy foods to taste, exotic plants to smell, hills to climb and waters to swim; hot sands to walk on, the sound of new languages, people to watch. What stayed the same was waking up next to my husband every day for two months. I know this wouldn't be unusual for many couples, but for us it was. I could sometimes see in my husband's face his surprise to see me there lying next to him.

'Shall we go home, Paul?'

So, to the surprise of our children and our friends, we returned to our comfortable Surrey home a month earlier than planned. We were both somewhat relieved.

The summer arrived rather late after lots of rain and grey skies.

'I'm feeling a bit stir crazy, Paul. How about a few days away, we could do some walking.'

'Not right now, I've got some meetings that I need to go to in London.' He wasn't forthcoming with any more information. I didn't want to give him the satisfaction of asking, so I got on with preparing dinner.

'I won't be here for dinner this evening,' he told me the next morning at breakfast.

'Anything interesting?' I said in a casual sort of way.

'Well it might be, I'm seeing some people about a possible job. Apparently there is a wish to bring more business expertise into the heart of government.'

I felt my spirits lift at the thought of an evening to myself. I had a few journals to catch up on. I have never lost my fascination with economic theory despite the fact that I gave up working over twenty years ago.

I was in bed by the time Paul got home. He slammed the front door and ran noisily up the stairs. I could see from his flushed, smiling face that he had had a successful evening. He couldn't wait to tell me.

'I've been offered an advisory role in the government, in the Department for Business, Innovation and Skills.'

'Congratulations.'

He seemed a bit embarrassed as he told me about his new position. I sat up in bed and tried to take an interest. There was a smell of whisky on his breath.

'Well so much for retirement!'

'You sound a bit out of sorts,' he said quietly, his enthusiasm tempered by my lackluster response.

'I expect I'm just tired.'

I could hear him singing in the shower and cleaning his teeth with vigour. He took off his suit, hung it up and joined me in bed, without his pyjamas, still buzzing with excitement. He wanted to make love, the first time for months. He was sexually recharged. I wasn't. I lay quietly thinking about this new direction our lives would be taking. Well a new direction for him. I was just staying in the same old role that I had been in for decades, a role that I resented. It didn't suit me, I felt that life was somewhere else. I had abandoned my career to be with Paul and now I was abandoned again as he went on to fresh pastures while I was left chewing the bitter cud of my earlier life choices, being bored and boring.

'Can't you sleep dear, I know I can't. I am too thrilled about this new opportunity.'

'Let's talk about it tomorrow, you can tell me all about it over breakfast.'

'Sorry love, but I have to go to a breakfast meeting with some ministers who I'll be working with.

Hot jealousy filled me and I had to resort to positive thinking to calm me down. *There must be some benefit in this for me. I must make some.*

I needn't have worried about the twice as much husband.

'I'll be late home so don't worry about dinner,' was a regular comment over breakfast. We slip into a new pattern, he goes into London every day and sometimes on weekends and I do what I have always done, which is nothing much.

Whatever he is doing in his new job suits him. He has energy, looks good and behaves in a charming and generous way. There are often phone calls, which he takes in his office. The half as much money isn't a problem. Strangely we have even more than when he was working for the company. My own life is pathetic. My only interest is going to lectures at The London School of Economics. It's not just the lectures. It's good to be out in the world and out of the house. One evening, during the coffee break, a handsome man of about my age approached me. I had noticed him looking at me during the last few classes.

'Hi, how are you? You've hardly changed at all. Long time no see.'

I didn't recognise him at first. I was still thinking about the lecture. When he told me his name, I remembered that we had been students at university at the same time.

'What are you doing these days?'

'Not much, how about you, George?'

'I'm a journalist.'

'Do you write about economics?'

'Sort of. I'm an investigative freelance reporter and write about a range of stuff, mainly in the business pages. You were the best student in our year. Surely you had some good offers?'

'Yes, but I drifted into marriage and family life. My husband did so much travelling that I gave up work to be at home with the children.'

'What a waste.' He didn't actually say it but it was clear from the expression on his face.

'Your job must be interesting, lucky you!' I really did feel envious.

'Fancy a drink? It would be good to catch up.'

I knew Paul would be late home as usual, so I accepted.

It was the first of many evenings. I enjoyed discussing the lectures with George and he even suggested that I might write an article with him. I was tempted but didn't feel able to commit myself. After a while, we stopped going to the lectures and just spent the evenings together. Sometimes we booked a room in a hotel. Meeting him had sexually recharged me and we made love often. One evening we were lying in bed together, drinking wine and talking about the world, politics, economics, business, anything and everything apart from our personal lives. Then George said that he had something to tell me.

'I met your husband last week.'

'How did that happen?' I asked, trying to hide my shock.

'I sat next to him at a dinner. We got into conversation. He'd had a few drinks and talked quite freely about his work.'

'Why are you telling me this?'

'Because he said something that I think you ought to know.'

'If you mean that he had an affair, I already know about that.' I felt angry just thinking about it.

'Yes, but he said that he had given up the love of his life.'

'For me. Yes I know. Let's change the subject.'

'No, not for you, for his career. An affair with a colleague doesn't go down too well in the corporate world especially if she is the wife of an up and coming politician.'

I felt my anger growing and tried to calm myself, although I could hardly pick up the glass of wine. My hand shook so much that I spilled some.

'You should have been the one with a career. You are much brighter than him.'

'Please stop, what's to be gained by this? It's all in the past.'

'I'm afraid it isn't. His former lover is now working for him. I've seen them together at meetings. I understand that she is doing research and reports to him.'

'Is she still married?'

'Yes, her husband is now a minister in the government. They have two grown-up children.'

'Does he know?'

'As far as I know, he doesn't.'

I felt as if something was crushing my chest. It crossed my mind that I might be going to have a heart attack it was beating so fast. I did some deep breathing to calm me down.

'Bastard, I hate him!'

'I don't blame you. If I were you, I would want to get my own back.'

'Just tell me how. He has everything, a great job and now, according to you, the love of his life as well.'

'You could take something away from him.'

'What?'

'He might lose this love of his life. If her husband found out and made her choose, I think she would stay with him. Perhaps even more important to him is his reputation. I think he is working towards an Honour and a seat in The House of Lords.'

'Typical, he can never get enough power. As his power goes up, mine seems to go down.'

'You could reverse that if you really wanted to. What have you got to lose?'

'Nothing, so what do I need to do?' I sipped my wine, it didn't taste of anything.

'Tell me what you know about his job with the company. Is he still on their pay roll? He seems to be part of a revolving door setup where ex-company high flyers get jobs in government and people in government move on to lucrative roles in companies. It's the way that companies can lobby government and find out information, which they can use to their advantage.'

'He hasn't broken the law, so what can be done?'

'I am a journalist remember. This could make a great story, especially as your husband's lover is the wife of an ambitious and unpopular minister. I have contacts who would happily publish this story. The public feast on sleaze, especially when it involves politicians.'

'I need time to think about it. It feels like a betrayal.'

'Haven't you been betrayed? All your talent and never an opportunity to develop it. Do you want to be dependent on him for the rest of your life?'

I got out of bed and dressed as if I was half asleep, in an atmosphere thick with confusion and indecision. George put his arms around me.

'Are you alright? I'll take you home.'

'It's OK. I'll call you tomorrow.'

For once Paul was home before me. He looked very pleased with himself. He got up from his armchair to greet me.

'Hello darling, was it a good lecture?'

'I didn't go to the lecture. I haven't been for weeks now. I've been seeing someone. I've been finding out far more interesting stuff, about you actually.'

His features sagged; he poured himself a whisky and sat down. I glared at him. He wouldn't make eye contact with me and cleared his throat.

'Do you want to tell me about it?' he asked in a quiet, resigned voice.

My anger melted away. Instead I felt the warm glow of power, the energy of it. I stood taller and smiled down at him.

'Your career and your need for power have always come first, Paul. That might be about to change.'

'What do you mean?' he said in a small voice.

'I could ruin your reputation and annoy your political colleagues.'

'Do you think I care about that?'

I couldn't hide my shock. 'So, what do you care about?'

'Love, I want to be loved. Not your sort of love, which is fine, and I thank you for it. I want the all-consuming kind of love. I had it once and gave it up. Now I have another chance and I won't give it up again.'

'She might give you up if I threaten to tell her husband.'

He put his glass of whisky on the table next to his chair. For a moment I thought he might do something violent but he just began to weep, gently at first then moaning and swaying back and forth.

'Thank you Paul, you've helped me make my decision. I don't care who you love. In fact, I'm glad it isn't me. I'm released from my obligations to you. I can be free to have what I want.'

He had gone quiet and still; he looked up at me. 'What's that?'

'The privilege of owning myself and coping with the dilemma of my own life.'

I poured us both a glass of whisky. Paul sipped his, he looked shrunken and defeated. I felt powerful and enjoyed it. I had never experienced it before. We went to bed, more or less as usual except that I knew that I had the power to ruin Paul's new career and his old love affair. I would never use it, I cared too much for the father of my children and he was a good man in many ways. Even making that decision was empowering. I decided that I would write an article with George. Then I slept, like a log.

I was woken up by my mobile phone ringing. It was Pat.

'How is it going? How are you coping with twice as much husband and half as much money?'

I decided to hold onto my powerful secret.

'It's just fine, how about you?'

The Scent of Hope

It was well worth the time and expense of coming home from his tour of Egypt. May was a good time to leave before it got too hot. Gentle rain had been falling as his carriage drove into Hyde Park. It smelt of England and home. He felt like cheering at his first glimpse of the palace of glass. The rain had washed away the dust and, as it gave way to sunshine, Prince Albert's Great Exhibition glass fantasy glittered among the trees, rising above them; an elegant structure engineered to perfection in iron, wood and glass. George smiled, it might not be the pyramids but it made him catch his breath in admiration.

He paid his entrance fee and wandered around the vast halls. He had come to see the Koh-i-Noor diamond and to meet up with some of his London-based friends. They had arranged to meet at the fountain in the centre of the exhibition hall. It couldn't be missed because it was twenty-seven feet high and made of four tons of pink glass. As usual he had dressed with great care, enlivening his outfit with a red and gold striped waistcoat. But compared with the Great Exhibition collection of furs from Russia, sumptuous tapestries from France and an Indian coat embroidered with pearls, rubies and emeralds, he felt drab and ordinary. Even when engaged in such pleasure pursuits, George never forgot about Riverton, his family seat in Dorset. So he looked around at the great new machines for anything that he thought could be useful for managing the acres of land and gardens. There was progress on view but sadly, only in some aspects of life in England.

He met his friends at the glass fountain. They greeted him with affection and asked about his recent trip to Egypt. He was reminded that whenever he was in England he was living a lie, a dangerous lie. Only a small, select group knew. What was acceptable in some European cities was a capital offence in England. There were no words to describe homosexual love, only a "death" sentence, which in a recent court case had been converted to transportation for life, which was another sort of death in his view. After enjoying the pleasures of the glass palace, George was looking forward to returning to the Riverton Estate where preparations for his visit had been underway for some time.

George's sister-in-law, Anna, looked around the dining room at Riverton, which was being readied for his "welcome home" party. The walls were already brilliant with the pictures he had sent from Egypt and Italy while on his grand tour. His stay this time would be brief. He had at last become an MP like his father before him. So he would be returning to London to his house in Piccadilly and his parliamentary duties. Whenever he was in residence, Riverton became besieged by visitors delighted to welcome back the handsome, extravagant and wild-living older brother and head of the family. Anna realised that she was glad when her brother-in-law left for London. All this excitement carried risks. He was still unmarried and there were rumours about his liaisons. He might get away with it in Europe, but not in England and definitely not at Riverton.

Like many others, Anna fell under the spell of George. Not only because of his striking good looks but also because he was the most interesting and entertaining man she had ever met. A polymath whose interest in archaeology took him to Egypt as well as Europe; he had many friends – artists, writers and poets, including Lord Byron. He dressed as befits a wealthy, handsome, artistic aristocrat. His hair was tawny blond and he often wore bright blue to accentuate his heavy-lidded eyes, which often sparkled with mischief and fun.

As usual the party surpassed even the highest expectations of the guests. A woman friend, Rosamund, had been invited down from London. Anna briefly hoped that she might become the next mistress of Riverton. It would solve the problem. Although George was very affectionate with her, Anna sensed that it was not to be.

A few days later he returned to London where he carried on with life with his society friends, clandestinely visiting homosexual brothels where they were able to meet male prostitutes and indulge in cross-dressing. His life was split into two halves: the serious often dreary work as an MP and the flamboyant, illegal shadow life, which satisfied his sexual needs. He knew that a few of his parliamentary colleagues who knew about his life regarded his behaviour as outrageous, although they admired his political acumen.

Sometimes the fear of blackmail caused him to rush off to Riverton but he could never stay away for long.

Engaging and charming, George was a popular man who was often invited to events by his fellow parliamentarians. He accepted a dinner invitation to The House of Lords with pleasure. He enjoyed serious conversation and political ideas fascinated him, even if the day-to-day business bored him. On occasion, after an intellectually satisfying evening, he ventured late to his old haunts. The thought was at the back of his mind as he enjoyed the dinner. The conversation turned to his most recent travels and he enjoyed a convivial evening. He even made a rather amusing if uninspired speech. The food and wine fell short of his Riverton cellars and kitchen but it was good to be in serious male company. Relaxing with a brandy he noticed a beautiful young man with one of his colleagues and organised an introduction.

'I hear that you have been in Egypt,' the young man said in a quiet voice. That was how it began.

He was the nephew of his colleague and was on a visit to London during a break from his studies at Cambridge University. George smiled with delight at the pale, delicate-looking student. What a wonderful evening, to be able to talk about his favourite topic to a beautiful young man. On the subject of Egypt, George spoke with great knowledge and love. The young man, used only to the dry, uninspired talks from the dons at Cambridge, was enchanted.

'It sounds like another world. I would like to go there myself.' Some colour had come to his pale face, his eyes shone and George felt a movement in his chest as if his heart were waking up.

'I have some of Egypt in my house. Would you like to see?'

Despite the late hour, they walked to George's house. William, the young man, kept up a steady stream of questions about Egypt. As usual, a light supper had been left on a tray in the library and they happily shared the food although they weren't hungry. William's enthusiasm and innocence charmed George. It was a world away from his usual encounters. They sat talking while the fire burned away to ashes.

'It's cold now and late. You must stay here tonight.' William smiled.

'Will you share my bed?' asked George, quietly. William nodded.

It was wonderful to burst out of the pent-up frustration and wallow in the post-orgasmic calm and sleepiness. George knew from past experience that the feeling of release wouldn't last long. It was soon replaced, as usual, by fear and trepidation and the avowal, made many times before, that this was the last time. It was a capital offence and he had too much to lose. He knew how weak he could be when tempted by beauty and the young man, William, was gently beautiful. When he smiled, George forgot the danger and thought only of the pleasure.

* * *

Despite his best intentions, he saw William whenever they could make it possible. Sometimes they met in Cambridge briefly, between their busy schedules. Their friendship and sexual bond grew. George no longer felt the inclination to visit his usual haunts, much to the annoyance of his society friends and former prostitutes whose attentions he had paid for handsomely.

Summer passed with many pleasures; they punted on the river in Cambridge and when William had time from his studies they made the most of London entertainments. To the surprise of George, William liked to visit music halls and the theatre. They went to Paris and Venice where they were openly together, to their mutual delight. During the autumn they saw less of each other, William was studying hard and George was spending a great deal of time dealing with the many new laws that were going through parliament. They were not able to be together over the Christmas period so each spent the time with their families. Christmas at Riverton was a time of lavish entertainment, many guests and traditional Christmas enjoyments, but in the absence of William they seemed more like chores to be endured. Both George and William were glad when Christmas was over and they could get back to their own lives, being together whenever it could be arranged. So it was with mixed feelings that George made his usual plans to be in Riverton in February.

'I have to go to Riverton for a while. I need to be there to supervise some renovations. I'll be back as soon as I can.' It gave him a sharp feeling of pleasure when William's face turned pale and sad. He had no idea how that memory would haunt him in the months to come.

Despite what some people would have described as a misspent youth with extravagant and wild living up at Oxford and extensive visits abroad, George took the job of managing his family estates very seriously. He shared the task with his brother, Henry. They were very different, although close. George was interested in beauty, Henry in money. Their very different drives and combined talents caused Riverton Hall to be one of the loveliest houses in England. It was filled with unique objects found during George's travels. Before William had come into his life, George had escaped regularly to Riverton especially after an "adventure" when he felt the need to put some distance between himself and temptation. This time he yearned for William and determined only to stay as long as necessary.

The journey by coach and horses was boring and uncomfortable. George passed the time reliving the intimacies shared with William. He arrived just as it was getting dark. His brother rushed out to welcome him.

'Is everything alright?' He was aware of the risks that George took when he was in London and was pleased to have him at home where he knew he was safe and away from temptation, at least for a while. George told him about William and his growing attachment to him. His brother's heart went out to him. He knew the limits that society imposed on their love affair and the risks they were taking. He felt anxious when he thought about what could happen if George's luck ran out. After dinner they sat together in the library, drinking brandy and listening to the homely noises of a fire burning in the grate.

'If anything happens to me, I want you to see that William is well provided for. Will you do that?'

'Of course, George.'

The next morning, George got up early to walk the estate grounds with his brother. There had been a thick frost and the air felt cold and thin. When the sun came up the frost began to melt and the sky was turquoise and cloudless. George liked to be at Riverton in February because of the snowdrops. He noticed one or two near the house, as if someone had dropped some pearl earrings. Alongside the paths, with the luscious ferns and wet grasses, they looked like a green and white lace cover over the dark earth. As the frost melted they glistened and so did George's eyes as he held back his tears. He was moved by their simplicity and purity, which seemed a world away from his London life of hypocrisy and deceit. He took deep breaths to absorb their cool, fresh scent.

'The gardeners have done a first-class job,' he commented to his brother.

From a distance the snowdrops looked like a homogenous snowy blanket. George knew that they were more intricate than they looked. Close up there were subtle differences and the head gardener was collecting as many different varieties as he could. Henry thought it was an unnecessary expense but to George the snowdrops were important. Every February he looked forward to seeing them, especially first thing in the morning. It set him up for the day. For years he had tried to understand why they had such a positive effect on him. The atmosphere in the early morning when the air was crisp and fresh slowed his breathing and calmed his jangled thoughts. So everyday, whatever the weather, he spent time walking in the grounds surrounded by his snowdrops, inhaling their exquisite, delicate scent.

'The scent of hope,' he explained to his brother. When the snowdrops had passed their best, he felt able to return to London.

He got back to his house in Piccadilly at the beginning of March. He couldn't wait to see William. Maybe there would be a letter saying when and where they could meet. To his surprise the mantelpiece in his study was empty. There were usually invitations to dinners, supper dances, or lunch with his colleagues. There was nothing. People knew when he intended to return so the empty mantelpiece took on a sinister significance. As he poured himself a brandy there was a tap on the door and the butler came in with a letter. He was disappointed that it was not from William but from the Prime Minister summoning him to a meeting at his residence.

"Do not enter by the front door", were the instructions. George felt sick and his heart raced as he wondered what was happening.

The Prime Minister did not keep him waiting long.

'I'm afraid that while you have been away at Riverton, there has been a great deal of gossip and accusations.' The Prime Minister looked down at his desk and not at George. His voice was grave.

'Your homosexual indiscretions cannot continue to be covered up George, too many people know about them and William has been tricked into betraying you. You know that this is very serious criminal activity. Even your powerful friends can't help you this time. You have to leave the country while you still can.'

George looked with sadness at his colleague.

'Is William alright? He mustn't be punished, he's only a boy with his whole life ahead of him. It's my responsibility.'

'William is alright, upset and very shaken of course. This is not of my doing nor is it my wish, George. However, you put too much at risk if you stay.'

'Thank you for your support, Prime Minister. I will make arrangements to leave at once.'

'Don't try to contact William. He has left London and Cambridge for the time being. It is better for both your sakes.'

As George left by the back door, he had tears in his eyes. He knew that he had to let William go. He hurried back to his house to make plans. He was not really surprised. On one level he had been expecting something like this. Part of the pleasure was the danger, until he met and fell in love with William. He cared deeply for him and didn't want him blackmailed or arrested. So he must leave as soon as possible. He knew that his brother would help. There were people he knew in Europe who were not offended by his homosexuality, so he planned to stay with them and then make his way to Italy. He had spent some of his grand tour there and liked it. The awfulness of his situation hit him properly when he retired to his bedroom. He stroked and smelt the sheets where William had been and, when he shut his eyes, all he could see was his lover and all he could hear were their whispers and shouts of pleasure.

He sent a sealed letter to his brother explaining the situation and left to take the boat to France. The sea and sky were grey and rough and he felt sick. He didn't know whether it was sea sickness or the loss of the best parts of his life that made him feel so low.

* * *

Spring was spent travelling around Europe and calling on friends he had made during his travels. As the weather improved so did his mood. There was much to see and enjoy. He sent letters to William inviting him to come to Paris and then to Nice. Although William replied, he did not acknowledge the invitations.

George arrived in Venice in June and rented a house on one of the smaller canals. He missed his house in London and his life as an MP. The ache for William was hard to bear.

William wrote a few letters about his life in Cambridge but reading them caused George to feel frustrated and angry. The letters seemed censored. He daren't allow himself to think of Riverton, and his snowdrops, it was too painful. There was plenty of sunshine in Venice in June. It sparkled off the water and the gold ceramics on the grand waterside villas. It satisfied, as it always had, his need to be immersed in beauty. There were parties to go to and young men who were pleased to come back to his villa afterwards. It was not the same as being with William but he made the best of it because there was no alternative. He had been declared an outlaw in England and was living in exile, but on some days he felt almost happy. There were many beautiful pictures and statues to enjoy, so some of his needs could be satisfied. At least here he could be himself and accept his sexuality. He soon brushed up his Italian so was able to enjoy the social life, the dalliances, fulfilling his sexual urges. But it was no longer what he really wanted. He longed for William, to see his intelligent face enquiring about this and that. Maybe he would be able to come and visit him. He would love to show him the beauty of Venice. He knew that it wouldn't happen. Rosamund came to see him and, enchanted by the picture galleries and sculptures, took a long lease on a nearby villa. They spent many pleasant hours together.

To fill his days he made drawings of architectural features he admired in case they could be used at Riverton. He bought sculptures and pictures to send home, always taking care not to reveal his whereabouts even to his brother. Only his lawyer in London knew precisely where he was. In July, Venice got hotter and on some days when he opened his windows there was a bad smell coming from the canal. It didn't help his mood. The friends moved on and he was bored by their replacements. Only Rosamund remained. He wrote regularly to his brother and relished the letters he received from him via his lawyer with news of parliament and especially of Riverton. From time to time his exile seemed unbearable. He was missing exciting times in London, especially in parliament. He felt that he had dishonoured his family by not carrying out his duties as an MP and abandoning his beloved Riverton. His brother now had all the responsibility of the family seat.

He dreamt about his snowdrops, their aroma so light and fresh in contrast to the heavy stench from the canals. His missed them.

Summer cooled into autumn and autumn dripped into winter. William stayed away.

'It's always raining here,' he said to his latest lover. 'The dank darkness makes me feel out of sorts.' The light was different. The sparkle had gone, replaced by dull grey mist. He liked mist in Riverton, he hated it in Venice. He spent a lonely Christmas and even the new, handsome young lover didn't lift his spirits. His exile took on a new meaning for him. He could cope with leaving England but he keenly felt the banishment from Riverton. He yearned to set eyes on William and stroke his delicate face. The pull of Riverton grew stronger as time passed. He was determined to return.

"Dear Henry", he wrote. "I must visit Riverton. Can you help?"

His reply came speedily.

"Do not even contemplate it, dear brother, it is too dangerous." It was a dark, sad day for George when he realised the true meaning of his exile and that it would be forever.

* * *

January was cold. Not the crisp, frosty English cold, but a soggy, misty, bone-chilling cold. He felt that his life was empty of love, of beauty, of hope. George could bear his banishment no longer. On a calm February morning, at the crack of dawn, a small boat landed on a deserted English beach. A man was there to embrace the older bearded man who climbed stiffly out of the boat. They clung to each other for a few moments, both in tears. Then they quickly walked up the beach and into the woods where horses were tethered. In less than an hour, George and his brother rode into the grounds of Riverton. They dismounted and the horses wandered away to the stables.

'I'd like to just walk the grounds, alone.'

'Be careful brother. Make sure no one recognises you.'

The snowdrops were there as he had pictured so many times during his exile. He could smell them, fresh, pure and sparkling from the morning dew; white, cool and beautiful, just like he had remembered. The air was intoxicating with their scent. He wished he could capture it so that it was always with him to give him hope.

He walked along the paths, sometimes bending down to examine their detail. There were even more than last time; the snowdrops seemed to go on and on like an earthly milky way. They faced no dilemma about being themselves. They were one hundred per cent snowdrops, absolute and true. How he envied them.

He knew that it was too dangerous to stay for long, so he filled his senses with their exquisite presence. He knew it might have to last a long time, maybe forever.

After a few days he made the long, arduous journey back to Venice. He had seen no one apart from his brother. He loved William too much to risk putting him in a precarious position. So with great fortitude he had made no effort to see him or tell him that he was in England. He felt safe in Venice. Rosamund was there to welcome him back. The joy he had felt on being with his snowdrops soon faded in the damp and cold of his villa. He hoped that his spirits would lift as the days lengthened but the weather was slow to improve and he caught a chill, which he couldn't seem to shake off. At the end of March he received a letter from William telling of his plans for an Easter visit. This was enough to raise George from his bed and his melancholy. Nothing was too much trouble for William. George counted the days until he arrived.

William was even more beautiful than George had allowed himself to remember. They spent their time exploring the waterways, admiring the palazzos with their delicate, exquisite frescoes. In the evening they sat on their balcony overlooking the canal and explored and admired each other. The days flew by and soon it was time for William to return to Cambridge. George felt something in him die.

As summer gradually arrived, the weather improved. The sun began to sparkle on the water and the gold ceramics. It made little difference to George, who seldom left his rooms. He began to feel unwell. He politely refused invitations and saw only a few close friends. Rosamund visited every day. He still wrote to his brother but did not have the emotional energy to write to William. Rosamund began to feel concerned.

'I long for William,' he told her. 'I miss Riverton, it is such a long time until the snowdrops come again. I fear that I will not be able to be there with them.'

* * *

Summer in Riverton was a busy time for Henry. So when a letter came from Venice he put it aside so that he could read it in the evening while savouring a brandy in the privacy of his study. He enjoyed letters from his brother. He sat at his desk to read it. It was not from George but from Rosamund.

"Dear Henry, I am sorry to give you the sad news that your brother died today."

Henry got up to shut the door. He would read the rest of the letter later. Through the window he could see in the pale evening light the lawns of Riverton and the garden that his brother had loved and inspired. When he closed his eyes, he could see the white clouds of snowdrops and his brother bending down to touch the tiny flowers and inhale their delicate aroma. The "scent of hope" he had called it. Henry made no attempt to stop his tears. George had made Riverton beautiful with his gifts of vibrant paintings, sculptures and fascinating artefacts from his extensive travels. When he was there the place came alive. When Henry realised that he would never be there again, he held his head in his hands and wept. George had brought love to Riverton, in the galleries filled with mirrors and pictures, and the gardens especially when carpeted with snowdrops. Who had given love to George? The love he wanted was forbidden.

When he had recovered somewhat from his tears, Henry resolved that George would be laid to rest among his beloved snowdrops. As long as the Riverton Estate continued, the snowdrops would be cultivated, cherished and shown to the world. A scent of hope for men like George and William.

The Unencumbered Woman

Unencumbered (defined)
(adj) not having any burden or impediment, not slowed down, or retarded, free to move, advance or go forward.

Chapter 1
KATHMANDU: MEET THE TREKKERS

It had been a day like no other for Caroline; hot, alarming and fascinating at the same time.

The powerful stench of spilled blood and freshly-killed animals hit her like a punch in the stomach. She just managed to fend off a wave of nausea and held onto her husband's hand. Hers was sticky with sweat.

'Why are they killing the goats?' she asked, looking to where they were penned.

'It's a Nepalese Festival,' he replied.

Several other people on the old rickety bus slowly moving around the polluted, festering rubbish-strewn streets of Kathmandu looked upset. Not for the first time, Caroline wondered why she had agreed to this trip. Even the hotel, although it looked charming from the outside with colourful columns and statues, was awful once you were in your room. Grey-looking sheets on the bed, threadbare towels and a noisy, intermittent water supply. Floating marigold petals in copper bowls didn't really compensate. Mike, her husband, was upbeat, savouring every aspect of the experience. He was determined to do the Royal Trek. One of his colleagues had done it last year and was still going on about it. So against her better judgement they had booked the trip. She usually did agree to his choice of holiday, she reflected. At least this time she had refused point blank to accept the longer trek. Four days was more than enough.

At Kathmandu Airport, when they had arrived the previous evening, Caroline had searched anxiously for other people with the same green and red tags on their luggage. When they were also wearing walking boots, it confirmed that they were on the same trekking holiday. She was relieved that the party of nine included four women and two seemed to be older than her. Relief made her hug Mike.

'I'm going to enjoy this trip, darling.'

'At this price, I bloody well hope so,' he said with a grin.

'I'll be glad when we start the walking,' said Jane, who was sitting in front of Caroline on the bus tour. 'I don't want to see another temple for a long time, I'm templed out.' Caroline smiled her agreement.

'Being in Nepal is a culture shock and I'm not sure whether to love it or hate it. Seeing poverty close up, the squalor, the air filthy with kerosene fumes, on one level it's horrible.'

'I just hope I'm up to it. I've never done anything like this before.'

'Neither have I,' said Jane. 'I've been thinking about this trip for years, so it had better be good.'

They got out of the bus near Durbar Square. It was a heady mix of colour and smells – good smells this time, of spices. People were haggling with the market traders, who were sitting with their jumbles of primary-coloured wares on striped blankets on the ground, selling clothes, shoes, or fruit and vegetables. There were lots of balloons and toys for children. Mike wandered off to look at another temple while Caroline and Jane strolled through the market looking for something special and unusual to buy.

'I'll see you back at the hotel,' called Mike as he joined another temple tour.

'How about going back to our hotel?' suggested Jane, 'We can get a cold drink and get away from this noise and crowds. I'd rather not wander about by myself, it still feels so strange.' The hotel was only a short walk from the square and had a small enclosed patio where they sat in the cool shade surrounded by pots of bamboo.

'I am impressed that you came on this trip by yourself,' said Caroline. 'I only came because Mike wanted to. It's not really my sort of thing. I'm too keen on my creature comforts. What made you chose this trip?'

'Because my life has changed, I don't have to stay in

the UK all the time if I don't want to. So I thought I would do something a bit adventurous,' said Jane.

'Good for you.' Caroline looked encouragingly at Jane.

'I've been living in Cornwall near my mother, she'd been ill for a while. I'm her only child so it was down to me to care for her. Sadly she died a few months ago. So now I can go where I like. It's a strange feeling after being tied for so many years.'

'I can see that. Do you have a job?'

'Well I did, I was a teacher. I inherited some money from my mother and a house. So I decided to give up working for a while. I can afford not to work now. I might even move, I was only in Cornwall because of my mother.'

'It sounds like an exciting time, a new phase in your life.'

'It is, but I feel unsettled. This trip will give me a bit of a breathing space until I decide what to do next.'

To her surprise, Caroline felt a moment or two of envy. She loved Mike and their two children but at times it felt as if she didn't have a life of her own. The children were both living away from home at university at the moment but they came home as often as possible, more than strictly necessary, Caroline thought. She felt guilty at how pleased she felt when they had to go back to university.

'Hi, did you enjoy the tour of Kathmandu?' It was Sandra, one of the other women in the party. They moved their chairs to make space for her to join them.

'I'm looking forward to starting the trek,' said Caroline, 'I've had enough of sightseeing and I've got information about gods and temples going in one ear and out of the other leaving no trace.'

'Well we're off to Pokhara tomorrow to get ready for the trek,' said Jane. 'Have you done this sort of thing before, Sandra?'

'Yes, I've been coming here off and on for years since my divorce. I find it very interesting. I haven't bought my return ticket this time. I might stay on longer after the holiday. I'll see how it goes.'

The trekking group were allocated their own table for dinner in the hotel. The three women – Jane, Sandra and Caroline – sat together. Mike sat with the other men, Max and Patrick, and the young couple, James and Joanna sat close together at the end of the table.

'I love your outfit, Sandra,' said Caroline. 'Did you buy it here?' She wore a bright pink long cotton shirt over orange trousers and a large scarf around her shoulders, orange to match the trousers.

'It's called a *kurta*, I got it when I was here last year. It's really cool.'

'It suits you,' said Jane. 'I envy you. I wouldn't have the nerve to wear it.'

At the other end of the table, where the men were indifferent to their clothes, the discussion was about the Royal Trek. Max had brought a map with him.

'Good man,' said Mike. 'Let's see what we are in for.'

James and Joanna were in a world of their own.

After dinner, the group were briefed about the next stage of their trip. They were advised to only bring with them what was necessary for the trek. Their remaining luggage would be stored at the hotel until they returned.

At the earliest opportunity, James and Joanna went to their room. The men ordered some beers and pored over the map of the trek and Jane, Sandra and Caroline sipped awful coffee and talked quietly for a short time before deciding that they needed a good night's sleep.

The next morning their luggage was locked away and, after breakfast, they were ushered onto a small bus for the drive to Pokhara. Their rucksacks were tied onto the roof of the bus and they settled down for the long drive. On the bus they spread themselves out to make the best of the window seats. Caroline sat by a window and Mike sat in the seat behind her. The party seemed to be in good spirits and there was some friendly banter as they drove out of Kathmandu. Sitting opposite Caroline were James and Joanna, the youngest members of the group. From conversations over the various meals they had taken together, Caroline had learned that this was their first trip together as a couple, although both of them were keen walkers and took pride in their levels of strength and fitness. She made a silent decision not to walk with them since she would be unlikely to keep up. Most of the banter came from the three men. Although they had been strangers to one another a few days ago, they were now bonding into friends, at least for the time being.

Like most trekking trips it had been timed to be after the rainy season. However, the rains had gone on for longer than usual and some roads had been badly damaged by mudslides. Even at the best of times the roads were rough so progress was slow. Caroline was glad that she wasn't driving. Occasionally she felt her stomach lurch. From where she was sitting, she could see that there was sometimes a steep drop at the edge of the road down into the river valley below. Despite the precipitous location, the roadside was edged with small shacks and she could see women bending over fires or little stoves cooking food, which was often for sale to passing drivers. In her mind it gave a new significance to the idea of "life on the edge". Whenever a vehicle stopped, the road was so narrow that there was soon a backlog of traffic. Caroline thought about her safe and comfortable life in London with Mike and the children and felt extraordinarily fortunate. Maybe it was worth the boredom. She couldn't imagine how anyone could go to sleep in the shacks for fear of ending up in the raging waters below.

Seven hours on the tortuous road with an occasional stop for refreshments, which they had brought with them, was a tiring but fascinating experience. Jane had moved from a window seat to sit next to Sandra.

'I hope you don't mind, Sandra, I just feel better.'

'Of course not, this sort of travel takes a bit of getting used to.' Sandra had already shown her experience in Nepalese travel. In her shoulder bag she had packed a notebook for writing a diary, a book of crossword puzzles, some headache pills, a pair of small binoculars and a large cotton scarf, which she wound around her head and shoulders. Jane felt comfortable under her wing and resolved to learn from her experience.

'I can see that you've done this before, Sandra. Why do you keep coming back?'

'It's a strikingly beautiful country and I like the people I meet here, especially in the villages. I feel I am properly away from home and all that stuff.'

'What do you mean?'

'Away from all the family stuff.' Jane looked interested so Sandra continued. 'I have two children, two sons, both married and three grandchildren. They take up a lot of my time, more than I want to give at this stage of my life. I've done bringing up children and I really don't want a repeat experience. Do you know what I mean? Do you have children?'

'No, I've never wanted to have children. Every time I got close to getting together with someone, when I explained that I didn't want to have children they moved on.'

'So you've never been married?'

'No. But I have had a special relationship. He was unusual in that he didn't want children either.'

'So what happened?'

'Sadly, he was killed in a car accident fifteen years ago and I haven't met anyone since. For the last five years I have been caring for my mother who lived in Cornwall, which is not the best place to find a partner. Now my mother has died I am free to go where I like. This is my first experience of this kind of travel.' Jane said with a smile.

'You still have time to meet someone.'

'I've been on my own for a long time now, Sandra. Not sure if I could make the necessary compromises.'

'You're probably right.' They sat together quietly as the journey continued.

The three men had also become quiet as the slow traffic extended their time of inactivity. Max, who was a G.P. in Surrey, had fallen asleep and David and Patrick were trying to play on a small travelling chess set, which was made difficult as the bus lurched about over the rough terrain.

Everyone was pleased when they could see that they were nearing Pokhara and within sight of the Annapurna range of mountains. Situated next to a lake it would be an ideal place to spend a few days and make sure they had all the kit required for their four-day trek. When they arrived at their hotel, they got off the bus with relief and were glad to stretch their legs as they wondered around while waiting for their rucksacks to be untied from the bus roof. Fortunately and surprisingly, none had fallen off.

'It looks better than the one in Kathmandu,' opined Caroline. 'It's got a swimming pool and the gardens are lovely.'

'Make the most of it,' said Sandra. 'Your next accommodation is in a tent.'

The food for dinner did not live up to their first impressions of the hotel. Nevertheless, they spent a pleasant evening talking and getting to know one another. Jane hung around Sandra until Mike moved to sit next to her.

'What do you think of it so far? Have you been trekking before?' Jane asked him.

'I've done quite a bit of walking in Europe but not with the extra excitement of camping. How about you?'

'I'm afraid that I've had a very sheltered life,' Jane said quietly. 'I have to say that I feel a bit scared, what if I can't keep up?'

'We have got sherpas to carry our stuff for us, I'm sure you'll be fine. Let me get you a drink.'

'That's kind but I won't, thank you. I feel a bit strange after that long bus ride. I think I'll go to bed.'

'We have an early start so that sounds like a good idea.'

Chapter 2
TREK DAY ONE: WOMEN TALK

The group had been instructed to be up early for the first day of the trek. They were taken from their hotel to the trekking centre to have breakfast and to meet the leader, Vishnu, and the rest of the team. Breakfast consisted of familiar food for a change: fruit juice, boiled eggs and toast. Mike nudged Caroline.

'Jane hasn't eaten anything. She just sipped water.'

'You alright Jane?' asked Caroline

'To be honest I don't feel too good, I had a bad night, I have an upset stomach. I couldn't eat anything right now.' She looked pale and anxious. 'I have taken some stuff so let's hope it works.'

The rest of the party appeared to be in fine fettle apart from a dry cough that Caroline had picked up in Khatmandu. They were told about the plan for the first day. They would be taken by minibus to the start of the trek, walk for three hours, stop for lunch and a break. There would be a further three hours, or maybe more depending on their progress. Then they would make camp, and have dinner cooked by the camp chef and staff before sleeping under canvas.

'Sounds like the adventure is about to begin,' said Caroline.

After a hearty breakfast eaten by some – and sips of water by Jane – they got back into the bus for the drive to the river where the trek would begin. Although the sherpas were to carry most of their belongings, each person was required to carry a small rucksack with spare clothes, suntan lotion, water, medicines and anything they would need during the trek. When they arrived at the river starting point there was a sudden silence as they looked out at the river they needed to cross.

'Bloody hell,' said Caroline. 'It really is a river. I thought it would be a stream we could just jump over; a bit fast-flowing isn't it.' The river wasn't exactly a raging torrent, but it rushed over rocks on the riverbed. Mike put his arm around her.

'You'll be fine. At least you'll start with clean feet,' he said with a grin. 'I can't wait to get started.'

They all got out of the bus and looked at Vishnu and the few sherpas. There was a bit of anxious chatter and repartee.

'OK, let's get going,' said Vishnu. 'The rest of the sherpas have gone on ahead, we'll see them at our lunch stop. You need to take your boots off and wade across the river.' Some in the group looked less than enthusiastic. Caroline walked towards a large rock and sat down to untie her boots. She walked into the water watching with intense concentration where she put her feet.

'Wow, it's cold,' she said in surprise. The rest of the group were now wading across the river.

Mike looked around to see how Jane was doing. She looked distressed and was moving slowly and gingerly.

'Are you alright Jane?' he asked. Jane didn't answer, just kept her head down picking her way across the large stones in the riverbed. She got to the other side and started to cry. Carol put her arm around her.

'I just can't do it. I feel terrible, I haven't had anything to eat for a few days. I just want to lie down.' Vishnu came over to see for himself what was wrong. Jane was shivering and pale.

'I think that you need to go back to the hotel and rest,' he said. 'You can rejoin us when you feel better.' Caroline could see that Jane looked relieved.

'Thank you. I don't want to hold you all up,' she said to the group, who were standing around looking concerned. A phone call was made, Jane was escorted back across the river by a sherpa and the rest of the group started their first day's trek.

It was all uphill on paths surrounded by shrubs. Once she got into her stride, Caroline began to enjoy herself. Mike, as she expected, was out in front with Max. She was happy to stay in the middle of the group and walk with Sandra. The pace was such and they were both fit enough to be able to walk and talk.

'Tell me about yourself,' said Sandra. Caroline felt pleased that someone was taking an interest in her.

'Well, I've been married to Mike for twenty-five years. We have two children, a boy and a girl, both now at university.'

'Lovely, but I was asking about you.'

'Oh, right. Well I did a degree in biology; I wanted to be a scientific journalist. In fact, I was for a while until I got pregnant. I really liked it. I often went to report on scientific conferences. I used to go abroad a lot, sometimes I would stay on after the conference, just for a week or so and explore a bit.'

'Sounds great.'

'What I really liked was that no one knew exactly where I was for a few days.'

'Before mobile phone tyranny I suppose.'

'Yes that's right. I made a point of doing it at least twice a year. When I think about it, I miss it.'

'Were you with Mike then?'

'Yes, but we were both working hard. Mike was a PE teacher. Not very happy, he didn't think his career was going anywhere. It was all a bit difficult because I was doing very well. I expect that I was in the right place at the right time. I felt that I needed to play it down a bit especially in front of other people. Mike didn't like people to know that I was doing so well.'

'Do you think he was jealous?'

'Who knows, it was all a long time ago. Then our circumstances changed when Mike got accepted into the army. It just suited him, especially the sporting opportunities.'

'What about your career?'

'We had to make some difficult decisions when he was posted to Germany. We decided that I would be an army wife and put my career on the back burner.'

'Was that a good decision?'

'It seemed so at the time. I enjoyed being a mother, at least most of the time. Eventually, I didn't feel good. I couldn't put my finger on what was wrong.'

'Is Mike still in the army?'

'No, he's gone back into education but on a freelance basis. He's doing very well; the army experience looks good on his CV and he gets some good contracts.'

'Do you have a job now?' Caroline took off her sunglasses and looked at Sandra.

'No. I do some voluntary work for a local school. It's not very challenging but I like being with the children. I feel the need to do something. Enough about me. How about you Sandra, what's your story?'

Sandra unwound her headscarf and shook out her hair. Caroline noticed the silver streaks and thought how attractive they looked. Although she was wearing sensible trousers she noticed that Sandra was wearing a full mid-calf-length bright pink skirt. She had a butterfly tattoo above her ankle, just visible above her sock.

'Easier to have a pee,' she said, when asked about her dress choice.

'I've done family stuff, got the small bank balance to prove it,' said Sandra. 'I'm divorced, have two sons and three grandchildren.'

'If you don't mind my asking, what went wrong in your marriage?'

'I felt as if I had to abandon my personal values and desires. My husband disliked me giving rein to my own wishes. He even wanted to control what I wore. I felt as if were just there as a base for the family; the family unit and all that stuff. Sometimes it was just plain awful, the children were tyrants. Eventually I realised that I was living a life of conformity and hypocrisy. Sorry if I sound as if

I'm over-egging it but that's how I felt.' Caroline nodded her sympathy.

'So then what happened?'

'I withdrew emotionally and sexually and my husband left.' They had both been so engrossed in their conversation that they hadn't realised that they were behind the rest of the group who had stopped for refreshments and to let them catch up.

'You've been having a good old chinwag, Caroline,' said Mike, as he joined her and offered her a drink of water. 'Anything interesting?'

'Just getting to know one another,' replied Caroline. She realised that she didn't want to tell Mike any more than that. They sat around resting and eating their lunch. To Caroline's surprise it was pizza.

'The sherpas give us food we are used to. They don't want us with gut rot,' said Sandra as she tucked into another slice. She got up to go to the toilet tent – a hole in the ground surrounded by a small privacy tent – and Caroline thought how sensible her pink skirt was. In her sixties, Caroline guessed, no attempt made to hide the grey hairs, Sandra seemed comfortable in herself. She looked as if she belonged trekking in the foothills. Caroline felt rather suburban in comparison with her blonde well-cut bob and expensive clothes. She had kitted herself up with all new gear from high-end shops and felt a bit embarrassed when she realised how posh she might seem to others in the group.

'OK time to go,' Vishnu encouraged them. The sherpas had packed the lunch equipment into big cane baskets, which they carried on their backs and were already well ahead. Although she had managed the trek so far, Caroline was not looking forward to the next couple of hours.

'I feel knackered already, Mike.'

'Come on love, you'll be fine,' he encouraged her. Within fifteen minutes or so, she had got into her stride again and looked around at the scenery with fascination. They passed through villages where they would pause briefly for a drink. To her surprise it was possible to buy a can of Coca Cola. Not usually a fan of the drink, in the particular circumstances it hit the spot. As the group passed local people, the women in their bright clothes, they would slightly incline their head, put their hands together and say '*Namaste*.' Caroline enjoyed responding in kind.

After four more hours of uphill walking, they reached their resting place for the night. As they got to a plateau the weary trekkers were thrilled to see a row of little tents already set up, the now familiar toilet tent and a table with chairs laid up for a meal. They were relieved to see, lying in a pile nearby, was their large packs carried up the mountain for them by the sherpas.

'Well done,' said Vishnu. 'There will be food in an hour or so. Just relax and enjoy the view in the meantime.'

Mike sat down on the grass and Caroline flopped down beside him. He took out his camera.

'I want to capture this, it is so special. Max, could you get a shot of us both with the mountains in the background please?'

Within the hour, as promised, hot food was produced. Not everyone had a good appetite and there was a request for anti diarrhoea medication from David. Max had come well supplied so passed some tablets to him with a bottle of water. There was a general good feeling that they had survived and in some cases even enjoyed the first day. Most of the group were tired, or were winding down as their adrenalin levels dropped and gradually they picked up their rucksacks, unpacked their sleeping bags and went to bed.

'I hope that I'll be able to sleep,' said Caroline as she snuggled down into her sleeping bag in the tiny tent.

'Of course you will, you sleep like the proverbial log normally.'

'That's the point, this isn't normal. It's dark and quiet, a little bit scary.'

'I'm here, there's no need to worry.' Soon Caroline's breathing indicated that she had taken Mike's reassurances to heart and was sleeping soundly.

Chapter 3
TREK DAY TWO: THE BEST LAID PLANS…

The tea provided in a tin cup by a sherpa tasted wonderful. Caroline had never had a cup of tea sitting up in a sleeping bag in a small tent before. It was warm, weak and there was no milk but it still tasted delicious. The fact that it was in the foothills of the Annapurna Range of mountains just made it even more extraordinary. She turned to Mike with a big smile and thanked him for suggesting that they do this trek.

'I had a feeling you would enjoy it, you always used to enjoy travelling.'

After the tea they were brought a small bowl of water for washing. To Caroline it seemed magical that in this seemingly isolated place they could drink tea and wash themselves.

'I've lived a small life lately, Mike; this is great, I needed reminding about the existence of the outside world.' They got dressed with some difficulty in the small space and went outside.

'What a way to start the day,' said Caroline, as she drank in the view of the snow-capped mountains

Breakfast was at the table. Vishnu outlined the plan for the day. As the sherpas cleared away the plates and folded up the chairs and tables, the trekkers went to their tents to roll up their sleeping bags and pack the small rucksacks that they would carry.

'Can you come and help me Mike, please? I can't get my sleeping bag into its pack,' said Sandra, who was in the next tent. 'They always seem to expand. It's a two-handed job.'

'Sure thing,' said Mike. Despite her problems with Mike, Caroline felt how lucky she was to be travelling with him. He was strong. He wasn't tall and handsome – in fact he was short, stocky and balding – but he was attractive. People liked his sense of humour and felt safe with him. He went off to help Sandra. Caroline reflected that someone needing him brought out the best in him, at least for a while.

According to Vishnu, the next part of the trek would be more challenging than usual because the late monsoon had caused some landslides. Everyone seemed to be in an upbeat frame of mind so they set off quite happily. The sun was shining. Sandra was wearing a lime green mid-length skirt with yellow leggings and black boots. Caroline thought she looked like an exotic bird in contrast to her more sombre knee-length cream shorts and long-sleeved linen shirt. As on the previous day, they walked uphill passing through villages and with views of the mountains. Because it was the time of the festival, even in small villages animals were being slaughtered. In the heat the smell was nauseating to Caroline. Sandra put a sympathetic hand on her shoulder.

'At least they eat the meat,' she said. Caroline nodded and sprayed more cologne on her neck.

The going got steeper and was made more difficult because the usual trekking path had been washed away.

Sometimes it was a scramble on all fours rather than a walk. They had looked at the map before they left camp and were aware that it was a hard day to come. From time to time the group stopped for a short rest and a drink. David bent down to attend to a spot of bleeding on his leg. Vishnu came over and explained that it was caused by leeches.

'Don't worry, just wipe this on it,' he said and gave him a bit of cotton wool soaked in something. 'These particular leeches don't carry anything nasty.'

By the time of the lunch stop they were all ready for a rest. A few in the group seemed to have lost their appetite. Caroline, however, was starving and tucked into whatever was provided. It was not hot and spicy, which was a relief all round. Mike sat next to her, he also had a good appetite.

'How are you doing?' he asked.

'Great, I'm surprised how much I am enjoying it.'

'Glad to hear it,' he said and kissed her on the neck. 'You even manage to smell nice here,' he said with a chuckle. 'I'm looking forward to tonight in our little tent, I hope we have some energy left.' Caroline smiled but said nothing. He always talked like that when he was feeling good. Of late, it was often just talk and no action.

Lunch was only a short break because they still had a long way to go to the overnight camp. There seemed to be mud everywhere, which made walking up stony steps to the villages treacherous. From time to time they stopped to look at the views, rice fields in the distance, mountains and more mountains. The order of the walkers changed. The two youngest members of the group, James and

Joanna, who had been out in front to start with, had now slowed their pace and were now bringing up the rear. Mike was in front with Max. They were deep in conversation. Caroline was relieved to see him entertained and adjusted her pace so she could walk with Sandra.

'He's a nice chap, your Mike,' said Sandra.

'Yes he is, but you can feel oppressed by nice people you know,' Caroline was surprised to hear herself say. Sandra stopped walking and looked at her.

'Of course you can, it's even worse somehow if they are nice. It's even harder to separate out because you lose as well as gain. That's why many people stay with it and think that the compromise is worth it.'

'I've compromised so much that it is now part of my normal behaviour, I don't even notice that I'm doing it.'

Mike and Max were so far ahead of the others that they weren't visible. Suddenly there was a shout and Max came rushing back to Vishnu.

'Mike has tripped on the mud. I think he may have a broken ankle.'

They all hurried towards where Mike was sitting on the ground with a look of distress on his kindly face, which had turned grey. They saw that he was in pain. Caroline rushed to crouch down next to him and put her arms around him. Vishnu and Max, who had immediately become the doctor he was in his regular life, examined Mike. He flinched with pain as they examined his foot and ankle. They helped him to his feet. When he tried to walk, even with their support, he couldn't put any weight on his left foot.

'Oh fuck,' he said. 'I have wanted to do this trek for such a long time.' It was crystal clear to all of them that he would not be able to continue the trek. Caroline was pale with shock and the rest of the group stood about, quietly uncertain about what to do or say.

'We'll have to get you back to the hotel and get this dealt with,' said Vishnu. He walked over to the small group of sherpas who were sitting on the ground while they waited for what would happen next. They spoke quietly together and then he came back to explain the plan to Mike and the rest of the group.

'We will get Mike down the mountain to a point where he can be picked up by a vehicle to take him back to Pokhara. The rest of you will need to wait here until we return. We will be as quick as we can but it will be a few hours.'

'I'll come with you, Mike,' said Caroline.

'It would be easier for us if you didn't,' said Vishnu. She looked at Mike.

'It's OK Caroline, just do what they suggest. You'll be back in two days. I just need to get this sorted.' Caroline felt torn between her sense of obligation to Mike and a surprising feeling of adventure. It was confusing. The decision was made easier when Sandra came over to her.

'I think it's best for everybody if you do as they say,' she said. So the decision was made. Mike was carried slowly, and with some difficulty, back down the stony steps and Caroline sat with the rest of the group to wait for the return of Vishnu and the sherpas.

They sat about, making desultory conversation for just over two hours until they returned. Since they had been delayed by Mike's incident the group seemed to feel the need to increase the pace of the trekking in order to get to the campsite in time for a meal. They were all a little subdued by what had happened. Caroline walked with Sandra, it helped her feel calm.

'Don't worry Caroline, he'll be alright. Things just happen sometimes to remind us that we aren't in control of everything in our lives.' They got into a steady rhythm of walking, which Caroline found helpful. She was so used to always being with Mike, especially in unusual circumstances, that it felt a bit scary to be trekking in the mountains without him. They reached another village where, as someone pointed out, there was a mobile phone mast. Several people turned on their phones.

'I suppose I should,' said Sandra. Caroline did the same. There was quiet apart from mobile phone tunes and bleeps while the group re-entered their world of family and work.

'I wish I hadn't bothered,' said Sandra in a low voice.

'Is anything wrong, Sandra?' asked Caroline.

'Yes, it's my grandson; he's been taken into hospital. Apparently he's not been well and has a very high temperature so my son and his wife thought that they had better be safe rather than sorry. So he's in hospital overnight for observation and tests.'

'That sounds like a good decision.'

'Yes, but I don't want to hear about it. It's not my responsibility. It's not my role any longer. I want to live my own life.' She removed her sunglasses to wipe her tears away. Caroline stayed silent because she didn't know what to say. So she put her arm around Sandra and gave her shoulder a squeeze. They continued their uphill trek.

'I hope Mike is alright, I'm going to be tired tonight. I didn't think he would be in the hotel and I'd be in a tent on a mountain by myself.' They both laughed to break the tension.

It was evening before the weary trekkers arrived at their campsite. There was relief all round to see the little row of tents set up in a tidy row, the toilet tent, a little distance away, and the table laid for the evening meal. Nobody wanted to stay up for long, they were all tired and happy to go to their tents. Sandra wondered who she could ask to help her roll up her sleeping bag in the morning now Mike wasn't around.

Caroline lay in bed trying hard to get to sleep and failing. She wasn't exactly frightened but she was definitely anxious. So she reached over to her rucksack, found her head torch and a book and read for a while until her eyes were tired and heavy. *I think I'm getting too dependent on Mike,* was one of her thoughts before she eventually drifted into sleep.

For Mike the journey back to Pokhara was painful and upsetting. His foot and ankle had swollen so that he had to take off his walking boot. It was distressing to be practically carried down the mountain by the sherpas who appeared to be half his size and weight. The shock of what had happened and its implications were just hard to take. He had been planning to do this trek for months and to crown it all he had been looking forward to an intimate night with Carol in the small, cosy tent. When they had eventually reached a road, a four-by-four vehicle had turned up to drive him back to Pokhara.

When he got back to the hotel, the trekking company had arranged for a doctor to come to the hotel and strap up his sprained ankle. Fortunately it wasn't broken. He couldn't fault the service and support he had been given. But he was not looking forward to a miserable few lonely days in the hotel.

After all the drama and disappointment, he decided that he needed a drink. He had been loaned a pair of crutches so he could manage to get about. The hotel had a lift, which was just as well since his room was on the third floor. With some difficulty he got himself to a seat by the swimming pool and ordered a cold beer. He was pleased to see Jane who was swimming up and down in the pool. In the shock of his fall he had forgotten that she was still in the hotel. There was no-one else around so she had it to herself.

'Good gracious, what's happened to you?' she said when she saw him take a seat and order a beer. She got out of the pool, wrapped a thin towel around herself and came over to join him.

'First of all, how are you? Are you recovered?'

'Yes thank you. I'm feeling much better.'

'Would you join me in a drink?' he asked, thankful for the company.

'Yes please, now tell me what happened.' He told his story.

'Oh dear, what a shame. I know how much you wanted to do this trek.'

'These things happen, the best laid plans and all that stuff.'

'Well I'm pleased to see you. I've been feeling a bit lonely here by myself. There are hardly any other guests. The pool is nice and I've had a few walks into Pokhara town centre, if you can call it that. But it's so quiet here. I've read the book I brought with me, so it will be good to have a bit of company.'

Mike smiled, the painkillers were working, he didn't look grey in the face any longer. Things were definitely looking up.

'I wish I could take you somewhere for dinner Jane, but I'm not used to crutches so I suppose we had better stay here, if that's alright with you.'

'It's fine, don't worry, I like the peace and quiet here, we practically have the place to ourselves.' Mike was surprised by how pleased he felt. It didn't exactly compensate for missing the trek, nothing could do that. In Jane's company he felt quite peaceful, unless it was the affect of the painkillers he had taken. He had always taken the attitude of making the best of the situation, he sensed with Jane around that it wouldn't be too difficult.

They decided to have dinner sitting outside where a tree with overhanging branches gave some shade. The flowers on it provided a refreshing smell and a cooling evening breeze helped his feeling of wellbeing. The accident had no affect on Mike's appetite and he and Jane enjoyed a pleasant dinner accompanied by a bottle of indifferent white wine.

'Are you very disappointed that you won't be able to finish the trek, Mike?' Jane enquired in a quiet voice.

'I suppose I should be, I've been going on about it for so long. How about you?'

'It has been a dream of mine. You have to have something to dream about when you live a tedious life. For years I felt responsible for my mother. Now she's gone, I feel a bit lost.' She took a sip from her glass of wine. When she put the glass down, Mike put his hand over hers. She looked up and smiled at him. 'Thank you, you're very kind.'

'Let's get another bottle of wine, it'll help us relax.' Jane nodded her agreement.

'I've always seen myself as independent. I don't know why I feel so vulnerable,' said Jane.

'Well you have been coping with some big changes in your life. It's a bit unsettling I expect.'

'It is. I'll no longer have any excuses.'

'What do you mean?'

'Well I can't blame anyone else for how I live my life now. It's up to me. I know that it should be exciting, but I feel a bit scared.'

'I'm not surprised,' said Mike and moved his chair closer so that he could put his arm around her.

'I feel a bit restless myself sometimes,' Mike surprised himself by saying. They started on their second bottle of wine and sat in the dark in silence.

'I just have a terror of compromise,' said Jane quietly.

'There's certainly plenty of that, especially when you are married and have a family.'

'How do you cope with it, Mike?'

'Because the benefits are worth it, at least most of the time. It's comfortable having a role, husband, father and so on.'

'Well I don't want the roles of wife and mother.'

'How did you manage looking after your mother, it must have been hard for you?'

'It was. I loved my mother and I hated being her carer. Now I am free, so I want to live my own life. I know that it sounds selfish but that's the way I feel.' Mike raised his glass.

'Good for you Jane, let's drink to that.'

By the time that they were drinking the last of the wine, Jane could hardly keep her eyes open.

'I feel sleepy. This is the first time I have felt relaxed since I've been in Nepal. I think I might have a good night's sleep tonight for a change.'

'Let me escort you to your room,' said Mike. 'Actually it would be helpful if you could escort me to mine. I think all this wine might not be good for my ability to manage these crutches.'

'It will be a pleasure,' said Jane with a smile. With some effort, Mike was helped to his room.

'I'm just down a few doors,' said Jane. 'Give me a knock in the morning and I'll help you down to breakfast. And thank you for a lovely evening.'

Chapter 4
TREK DAY THREE: A DEVELOPING RELATIONSHIP

After a surprisingly restful night, Caroline was wide awake and raring to go when the sherpa brought her morning tea. She dressed and wriggled out of the little tent. It was a lovely day, with a deep blue sky and views of snow-capped mountains. She sat at the table for breakfast with Sandra on one side and David on the other. She had noticed that he had been rather quiet during the trek so far, so maybe he was on the shy side. In such a good mood herself she decided to find out something about him.

'How are you finding it, David?'

'Oh fine thank you. I hope your husband will be alright. Such a pity, he told me how much he had been looking forward to this trip.'

'Yes it is a shame.' Caroline realised that she hadn't really given Mike much thought and felt guilty and embarrassed. She had overheard David talk about his work as a marine engineer so decided to ask him about it.

'I fix boat engines,' he said. 'I work on the south coast where there are plenty of marinas and well-off yacht and motorboat owners. It's a good job. I work for myself so it's flexible. That's why I can take time out for this trip. My wife didn't want to come, so I decided to come anyway.'

'Didn't your wife mind?'

'To be honest, I didn't ask her. She never wants to do anything that I want. We have a boat, she never comes on it. I would just like to get up one day and hear her say, "It's a lovely day, let's go on the boat," but she never does.' Caroline didn't know how to respond so she sipped her tea and smiled.

Vishnu outlined their plan for the day while they were finishing breakfast. Part of the trek involved going down some steep slopes, he explained, and that care was required because there were quite dangerous edges.

They set off. The group seemed to be in good spirits and chatted together. As they passed local villagers walking to and from their homes they returned their greeting of '*Namaste*' holding their hands together and gently inclining their heads. Caroline was enchanted. She had been assured that Mike was well looked after and relaxing in the hotel in Pokhara. So she quickly got into her walking stride and walked with Vishnu. He spoke excellent English and told her about a project that he was involved with which raised money to help young people learn useful and saleable skills.

'That's excellent,' she said. 'What sort of skills?'

'We have some old motorbikes so that they can learn how to work on engines and mend the bikes. The young women are taught how to make bags and cushions to sell to tourists. It helps keep them safe.'

'Safe from what?'

'Men.' Caroline was again rather lost for words. They walked on for a while in silence. She slowed her walking pace and slipped to the middle of the group where she walked on her own. She felt something she couldn't quite put her finger on. Something she hadn't felt for a long time. When she thought about it, it was since having the children. For years she had made her family home a sanctuary for the family and herself. Lately, she realised, it had felt more like a prison. That was it, now she felt free. It was frightening and exhilarating at the same time. Sandra slowed her pace to be in step with Caroline.

'You alright Caroline? You've gone quiet.'

'I'm great Sandra, thank you. Just thinking about things.'

'Anything you want to share?'

'I just feel so liberated. I haven't felt it for years.'

'It takes some getting used to. All I can say is, enjoy it while you can.'

'You seem a bit subdued Sandra, how are things with you?'

'I can't stop worrying about my grandson. I can't do anything about him, so why did they have to tell me?'

'That's what families are like. They expect you to abandon yourself in order to be part of it.'

'I'm trying to escape from these old roles. I'm too old for them now. What time I have left I want to be for me.'

'I understand that Sandra, I'm beginning to feel it myself. Are we being selfish?'

'No we're not. My ex-husband often made unilateral decisions without checking it out with anyone. Nobody thought that he was selfish. We are just too passive, always accommodating others.'

'Perhaps I'm going to change my ways,' said Caroline with a giggle. 'Live my own life for a change.'

'Well good luck with that,' said Sandra.

'Don't sound so grim, it can't be that difficult.' Sandra didn't reply.

They walked on for two hours with a brief stop for refreshments. When they resumed the trek it was down some very steep and slippery stone steps. On one side there was a steep drop. Some of the group were a bit scared and held back so Vishnu asked the sherpas to stand at the edge of the steps to help them feel less anxious. Caroline had resumed her position in front with Vishnu, although they often had to trek in single file when the steps became very narrow.

'Bloody steps,' shouted David, as he lost his footing and slipped down onto his backside. A sherpa moved towards him to help him up. In the quiet the shout seemed loud.

'Don't touch me, leave me alone. It's your fault you were in my way, stupid man.' The group were silent with shock for a moment. Then several people began to speak at the same time, pretending nothing had happened. At the bottom of the valley was another stream which they needed to cross. When Caroline saw the rickety rope bridge she felt her pulse rate increase. Since her menopause, her balance had been deranged. It was gradually improving but it wasn't as good as it used to be. Vishnu saw her alarm.

'You'll be fine Caroline. I'll be walking right behind you. You won't fall.' She decided to be one of the first to cross so that her nervousness had no time to develop further. When she got to the other side the sense of achievement was such that she wanted to cry with relief and pride. The others crossed with varying degrees of confidence. Sandra just picked up her skirts and seemed to glide across. The last to cross was David who shouted at the sherpas as they took his rucksack and walking poles.

When he got to the other side Sandra said gently, 'They are only trying to help, David. What's the matter?'

'Nothing,' was his surly reply.

The sense of relief in the group showed itself by louder than usual talk and banter as they walked on to the lunch stop. They passed through villages where the children walked along beside them. Sandra had brought little coloured pencils and notebooks which she gave to them. Caroline wished she had something to give. Despite their rough-looking living conditions, she thought that most of the women looked beautiful in their colourful clothes. She had read that most Nepalese people get their living from the land. The literacy level for women was lower than for men, and was less than 50% . The idea of being unable to read made her feel sad.

'We are so lucky,' she said to Sandra.

'I don't think we should judge, we have no idea, we can only see things from our perspective. Keep an open mind, Caroline.'

'I hope Mike is getting on alright,' said Caroline, realising that she had enjoyed the day so far and hadn't missed him at all.

Back in the hotel in Pokhara, Jane and Mike sat together for breakfast.

'We can't sit here all day, Jane,' said Mike, pouring himself a second cup of coffee.

'Well what do you suggest? You can't go far with those crutches.'

'I can organise a driver to take us on an excursion for a few hours. How about that?'

'Excellent. I'll see if we can get a packed lunch so that we can have a picnic somewhere beautiful.' They smiled at one another. After Mike had finished his coffee he phoned the tour operator's office. 'A driver will pick us up in an hour,' he said. Jane went to the kitchen to organise the packed lunch.

'I need to get myself ready so I'll see you at the hotel foyer in an hour,' she said. Back in her room, Jane packed her small rucksack with things for the day and chose her clothes with care. She wanted to look good. The thought of spending the day with Mike had lifted her spirits. She felt confident being out and about with him. The trip was looking up. She was feeling well again and excited about their excursion.

Both the car and driver looked as if they had seen better days. They set off towards the hills of Naudanda, driving past rice fields, with views of the snow-capped Annapurnas.

'This is lovely, Mike. I was beginning to regret my decision to come on this trip. Now I'm glad I did.'

'So am I – glad you came I mean,' said Mike as he put his hand on Jane's arm. She liked how it felt and just kept her arm still and smiled. They drove through a few villages. Their driver told them about the festival of Desain and explained that the high bamboo poles were swings for the children. Jane felt a mix of excitement and safety. For all her supposed independence she was aware that she would not have felt so comfortable exploring on her own. There was something about sharing the experience that heightened it. Because she felt safe, she felt able to engage with the adventure. Because of his injury, Mike was unable to walk far. The driver took them to a place where they could eat their picnic lunch. He took a small table and two chairs from the car boot and set them up. He left them alone and said he would return in an hour.

Jane unpacked the picnic.

'I'm actually hungry, the first time for days,' she said, as she tucked into some bread and cheese. 'I was beginning to think I would never feel hungry again. It's such a relief.' They drank some beer and toasted each other.

'I felt so pissed off when I fell,' said Mike. 'I thought my Nepalese adventure was over. But it isn't. It's just a different kind of adventure.' Jane felt her heart rate increase.

'I feel a sort of excitement myself,' said Jane. 'I sense that my life is going to be different.'

'Of course it is. You are free now to do your own thing.'

'The problem is finding out what that is. I've been encumbered for so long that I have forgotten what I want, if I ever knew.'

'You need time, Jane,' said Mike gently. 'There's no rush.'

'I'm a bit scared really. If I get it wrong there is no-one else to blame.'

'You won't get it wrong.'

When they finished their picnic, Jane packed things away while they waited for their driver to return.

'That was lovely, the most ordinary food can taste wonderful when you haven't eaten much for a few days,' said Jane.

Mike looked at her. He could see she felt relaxed. Her face had softened so that she looked young and vulnerable.

'I think the company and surroundings help.'

'Of course they do.'

The driver packed the table and chairs into the car boot and they got into the back of the car.

They sat close together. Jane felt sleepy despite the bumpy ride. Mike saw her eyes closing.

'Why not have a little nap,' he said and put his sweater under her head.

She slept until they got back to the hotel.

'Jane, we're back.'

'Have I slept the whole time? You know that's my first proper sleep since I've been here.'

'Then you need it. I suggest you go and have a bit more rest and we can meet for a drink before dinner.'

Jane chose a short black dress for her rendezvous with Mike. Her sleep seemed to have improved her appearance. Usually very self-critical, she acknowledged that she looked good. The tension of being abroad in a strange country had melted away in Mike's company. She made herself be a few minutes late and enjoyed his appreciative appraisal when he saw her arrive.

'You look great.' They sat on a cane sofa and ordered their drinks from a waiter. A new group of tourists had arrived while they had been on their picnic. The hotel was lively.

'What's it like here, have you had a good day?' asked a woman sitting at the next table.

She hadn't noticed Mike's crutches.

'Yes thank you,' replied Jane with a smile. It occurred to her that the woman thought that she and Mike were a couple. A new experience for her. She realised that sometimes when on her own she felt a social misfit. While she had been a carer for her mother it had seemed fine to be without a partner. Now, it felt less comfortable, more scary. She began to understand why many people found it difficult to be alone. Perhaps she had needed her mother as much as her mother had needed her.

After two glasses of white wine and Mike's two glasses of beer, they moved into the dining room to order dinner. They were treated by the other diners as a long-established couple. Neither of them said anything to challenge the assumption. To see them with their heads close together, clearly enchanted with one another, they could have passed for a honeymoon couple. When it was dark they left the dining room to find a seat outside where they sat and enjoyed the smells coming from the plants in the garden. As the other hotel guests returned to their rooms, Jane and Mike sat quietly talking. It was very late before they went to their separate rooms.

Chapter 5
TREK DAY FOUR: CHANGING PERSPECTIVE

After only three days, Caroline felt as if she had been trekking in the foothills for ages. The morning mug of tea brought to her tent was an anticipated pleasure and a fine way to start the day. The fact that it was the last day of the trek was a source of mixed feelings.

'This is our last breakfast in the mountains,' she said to Sandra at the breakfast table. 'I feel as if I am just getting going and now it's almost over.'

'Well, isn't that up to you?' replied Sandra. Caroline felt her heart rate increase at the thought. She didn't reply and Sandra gently squeezed her arm. It was another clear and sunny day, even at eight o'clock in the morning it was hot. Vishnu explained that the trek was short today and that they would have finished it by early afternoon. There were looks of relief on some faces and touches of sadness on others.

Sandra and Caroline helped each other roll up their sleeping bags, it was easier with two people.

The group set off on their last day's walking in good spirits. The order of walking changed from time to time. There was a lot of talking, the group were close after spending three days walking and living together. Caroline sought out Vishnu.

'I would like to do something for women in Nepal,' she said. 'I hope that doesn't sound patronising.'

Vishnu smiled, 'Quite often people feel like that when they visit,' he said. 'Especially women.'

'Does anything come of it?'

'Not as a rule. They forget all about it when they get home.'

'What a shame,' said Caroline. 'I can understand why that happens, life takes over, family take over, obligations take over.'

'Of course,' said Vishnu. 'I don't blame them, it's understandable. We will be passing through a village where there is a school run by a woman. You could speak to her.'

'Does she speak English?'

'Yes, she lived in England for a short while.'

'That's great. I would like to speak to her please if it can be arranged.' Vishnu nodded his head. Caroline caught up with Sandra, to tell her what had just been said.

'That should be good Caroline, any chance I could join you? I would find it interesting.' Caroline smiled and nodded her agreement with a sense of relief. Within the hour the group were walking through a village where signs of the festival of Desain were much in evidence. In the heat, the smell of the animals was intense and Caroline sprayed a scarf with scent and put it round her neck. Children were playing on the high bamboo swings. A young woman wearing a bright orange dress was watching them. Vishnu called to her and she came over to speak to him.

He spoke for a while in Nepalese. She responded by nodding and smiling. Then he introduced Caroline and Sandra who made the traditional *Namaste* greeting.

The children were enjoying their lunch break, explained the teacher. Then they would be back to their classes until six o'clock.

'There seem to be more boys than girls,' said Sandra.

'Yes there are. Children are used as cheap labour to work for their parents and some of the girls are married.'

'They are only children. How can they be married?' asked Caroline.

'It's against the law. But it happens anyway. Sometimes to the girl it seems like the least worst option.' Sandra saw that Caroline was near to tears and put her arm around her shoulder.

'Don't judge Caroline, it's not helpful,' said Sandra.

'Do the families have to pay to send their children to school?' asked Caroline in a whisper.

'Not this school,' said the teacher. 'But they have to buy pencils, paper and a uniform.'

'It must be hard for them,' said Sandra. The teacher nodded.

Vishnu, who had listened in silence while the women talked, looked at his watch.

'We have to go, the bus will be waiting for us. We are due to be back at your hotel this afternoon.' The women thanked the teacher and walked slowly back to rejoin the rest of the group. The walk continued. Caroline and Sandra walked at the back of the group. Caroline turned her head to look back at the children as the teacher ushered them back into the schoolroom, a low hut with a tin roof.

'I know what you mean when you tell me not to judge,' she said to Sandra. 'It just makes me feel so sad. At least I chose to get married, I chose my encumbrances and I had a life of my own before that. Those poor girls.'

'I don't think we appreciate our freedom,' said Sandra. 'To think that we chose to be encumbered. Why do we do it?'

'Because we are too scared to live our own lives. It's easier to do what everybody else does, to conform. We have children then use them as a distraction so we don't have to think about what to do with our lives.' They walked together in silence, each managing their own thoughts and feelings. After two more hours of gentle downhill walking, the group came to another village where the bus belonging to the trekking company was waiting to take them back to their hotel in Pokhara.

'Well done everybody,' said Vishnu. On the bus there was a lot of banter and laughter as people relaxed. They had survived the trek. They had done the Royal Trek, something to tell their friends and family with plenty of photographs to prove it. Caroline and Sandra sat together separate from the rest.

'I wonder how Mike has got on,' said Caroline quietly. She realised with some guilt that she hadn't missed him. After the first few hours, as soon as she knew that he was safely back in the hotel, she hadn't even thought about him.

'I'm sure he has been fine,' replied Sandra.

'You're right. He always lands on his feet whatever.' She knew that she sounded resentful. Sandra sat quietly and put her hand on Caroline's.

Back at the hotel the group got out of the bus. A few of them went to their rooms. Caroline, Sandra and Max walked to the swimming pool where they could see Mike and Jane sitting at a table under an umbrella enjoying a drink. Jane had wet hair and was wrapped in a towel. Mike was wearing shorts and a t-shirt. His crutches were leaning up against a chair. They were engrossed in conversation and didn't notice them arriving until Caroline greeted them.

'Hi, we're back.' They looked up, seemingly reluctant to be interrupted. Mike stood up helped by holding onto the table. Caroline gave him a hug. He felt different, not leaning into her in his usual way.

'Have you had a good time?' he asked.

'Yes it was great, we missed you both.' Caroline knew she was lying. 'Have you been OK here, how's the ankle?'

'We've been fine, taking it easy. Good job Jane was around to keep up my spirits.' He smiled at her. Caroline had known Mike a long time. She could see his longing for Jane. There was no need for words.

'I think I need a proper shower,' she said. 'I'll see you guys later. Coming Sandra?'

They walked over to the hotel.

'Well Sandra, what do you make of that?'

Chapter 6
CAROLINE MAKES A BREAK

When Caroline and Mike were eventually alone in their room, she suggested that they open a bottle of wine and have a chat.

'Sure, but is there anything wrong? You enjoyed the trek didn't you?'

'Yes I did Mike. I didn't think I would after your accident, but I did.' She took a long drink of the wine. 'I thought that I would feel guilty about it, but I didn't.'

'It's alright Caroline, I had an OK time here in the hotel, better than I thought it would be.'

'That's because of Jane isn't it?' Mike blushed and said nothing.

'You don't have to say anything, I could see from the way you were with her.'

'What do you mean?'

'There was a warmth and a kind of tension between you. I remember that we had it in the beginning,' she said. 'It's sad when it goes even though it's compensated for by other things.'

'Such as?'

'The children and all the mutual network of family and friends.' Mike said nothing and poured more wine for them both.

'I had an interesting experience today, Mike. I went to a school in one of the villages. Not as many girls as boys but some. I felt something that I haven't felt for years.'

'What was that?' Mike asked in a small voice.

'Motivated. I felt that I wanted to do something, to help. It was an exciting thought.'

'I don't really know how to respond to you right now. I'm feeling knackered. Can we talk about it tomorrow?' Caroline nodded.

'It will be good to sleep in a proper bed.' She wondered if Mike had his mind on the sex he had been looking forward to in the tent. He didn't. She was relieved. She felt unsettled and needed to get her head around what she wanted and not just go along with Mike's agenda. Since she realised that she hadn't done that for years, it was going to take a bit of an effort.

'Let's talk about things in the morning,' said Caroline. But Mike was already asleep or pretending to be. When she shut her eyes she could see the school and the children. *I'm going to do something*, was her promise to herself.

The next morning, Caroline was up first. When Mike roused himself she was already up and dressed and eager to go down to breakfast.

'You go on ahead, I'll be down in a bit,' said Mike from his bed. Neither of them mentioned the discussion of the previous evening. Caroline joined Sandra at her table. She poured herself some coffee and helped herself to a modest breakfast.

'I've been thinking about that school. I'd like to go back and see it again, talk to the teacher. Do you think Vishnu could organise it?'

'I expect so. But we are supposed to be travelling on to the national park today.'

'Well I could always come later. Do you want to come to the school with me? You can see the park another time.'

'I think you need to speak to Vishnu before you get all excited about this,' said Sandra. 'What about Mike, what does he think about your plan?'

'I don't know. I haven't asked him,' said Caroline and couldn't help a broad grin. 'I can't spend any more time accommodating others. I need to be more proactive and self-determining.'

'Wow,' said Sandra. 'What's come over you?'

'It's about time I made some choices in my life. I haven't done it for so long that I'm out of practice. The children have left home now so I don't have them to worry about.'

'And Mike?' asked Sandra.

'I've given probably the best years of my life to our marriage. But it isn't enough any longer for either of us.'

'Has he said that?'

'Not in so many words, he's too kind. Did you see the way he was with Jane when we got back yesterday?'

'There did seem to be a bit of an atmosphere. Has he said anything?'

'No. He's too conventional. I don't want us both to be doomed to a life of conformity and hypocrisy. So I have to do something.'

'Good for you, it's a brave decision and a risky one. There may be no going back.'

'I get that. Personal freedom doesn't come without some anxiety.'

'And responsibility,' added Sandra.

'Bring it on, it's about time I created my own life and identity.' They ate the rest of their breakfast in silence, each thinking about the implications of personal freedom.

When Vishnu appeared to discuss the next part of the trip with the group, Caroline took him to one side and asked if he could arrange for her to return to the school. He made a phone call.

'It's arranged, a car and driver will collect you at about eleven o'clock. By the time you return we will have left for the The Royal Chitwan National Park. I can arrange for you to come on a bus to join us, but it won't be for a few days.'

'OK,' said Caroline. 'I'll just see if Sandra wants to come with me or go to the park.'

'I've already been to Chitwan,' said Sandra. 'I'll come with you to the school.' Caroline felt excited and pleased to have the company and support of Sandra.

'Thank you Sandra, I felt a bit scared of going by myself. I had better go and explain the situation to Mike before he comes down to breakfast.'

'Caroline, what is this all about? Don't you want to go to Chitwan?'

'Yes, I'll be joining you in a few days. I want to go back to the school.'

'Why?'

'I'm not really sure. If I don't, I know that I will regret it. Sandra is coming with me. You will be able to spend time with Jane. It works for both of us.' Mike looked away.

'I suppose so, if that's what you want. I had better go and get some breakfast, we'll be leaving for Chitwan soon.'

'I'll take your bag down for you, Mike.'

At eleven o'clock, Caroline and Sandra were picked up and driven away to the school. They were dressed for trekking since the last part of the journey to the school would be on foot. Vishnu had arranged for a guide to show them the way. Caroline was delighted, she didn't want to get lost in the foothills. Half an hour later, a bus arrived at the hotel to take the rest of the party to the national park. Jane helped Mike by holding his crutches while he pulled himself up the steps into the bus. She got on behind him and sat next to him for the journey.

'Are you alright, Mike? What's Caroline doing? Why isn't she coming with us?'

'I don't really know. She and Sandra have gone back to the school. When she really makes up her mind about something, there's no way of changing it.' Jane said nothing and moved closer.

Chapter 7
GETTING CLOSER

The bus journey to Chitwan National Park didn't last long enough for Jane. Sitting next to Mike felt safe and exciting. For the first time in her life she felt part of a couple and, to her surprise, she liked it. When they weren't deeply engaged in discussing their lives, they were dozing, her head resting on his shoulder. It was late afternoon when the bus stopped outside the lodge where they were staying for the next four days. They got out of the bus and stood about while their luggage was piled up outside the front of the lodge. Mike had decided to try managing without the crutches and use his trekking poles.

'I'm bloody glad to get shot of them,' he said to Jane. 'I'll be back to normal soon. In some ways anyway.' Jane moved away and looked for her luggage. The group checked into the lodge and were given their room allocation.

'When will Caroline and Sandra come?' asked David.

'Tomorrow or the next day. When she's done what she needs to.'

'Women,' said David. 'You can never understand them.'

'See you at the bar later,' said Mike.

'Sure. Do you need a hand with your luggage?'

The group assembled in the bar to be told the various options and trips available for them during their stay at Chitwan. Mike felt that he wasn't up to a forest walk just yet.

'I'll stay and keep you company,' said Jane. The rest of the group set off for their evening walk and Jane and Mike sat in comfortable chairs on the outside terrace. Mike ordered a bottle of wine and they resumed their discussion from the bus journey. From time to time, Mike checked his mobile.

'Sorry Jane, but I'm expecting a call from my son.'
'It's fine Mike, I can see that you are a family man.'
'What does that mean?'
'Well you like being a husband and father.'
'I've never really thought about it. It's what you do.'
'You don't have to. I didn't.'
'Have you ever had any regrets about not having children?'
'None. It would have been too overwhelming. I need time for myself.'
'I have time for you, Jane. I want you just as you are. How did you manage being the carer for your mother? That must have taken a great deal of time.'
'I thought that I didn't have a choice.'
'But you did, you chose to do it.' Jane didn't reply for a few minutes. Mike looked at her.
'I suppose you are right. I took the easy way. Perhaps I don't really want freedom. It makes me anxious.' They drank their wine and Jane changed the conversation.
'What shall we do tomorrow? Do you fancy the elephant safari?'
'Great, I should be able to manage that. It doesn't involve much walking I presume.'
They sat working through the bottle of wine until the

rest of the group returned from their forest walk. Jane noticed that his son hadn't called.

'I'm off to bed. See you all at breakfast,' said Mike. Jane felt disappointed. She didn't feel ready for bed so stayed with the rest of the group, chatting about what they had seen on the walk. There was a general consensus that the elephant safari sounded like an experience not to be missed.

Mike and Jane were the first to get to the start point for boarding the elephants. With help from Jane, Mike got up the steps, onto the platform and then into the wooden crate on top of the elephant. There were mattresses to sit on. Four people rode each elephant that was driven by a mahout, a young boy. Jane clambered on board and sat next to Mike. Their legs dangled down but they were held in place by the sides of the seating structure.

'I hope this is worth it. It's bloody uncomfortable,' said Mike. 'You alright Jane?'

'I'm fine,' said Jane in a small voice. She was holding on to the side of the crate. 'I hope it doesn't go on for too long.'

They set off through the long grassland, hoping to see the famous one-horned rhinoceros. They slid about a bit in the crate as the elephant got into his stride. Jane was pushed against Mike. He took her arm and held her in place, close to him. The mahout drove the elephant towards the river. As the elephant walked down the bank into the river, their platform sloped downwards and Jane felt her heart rate increase. The platform was firmly attached, nevertheless, Jane was pleased when they came out of the other side of the river. The mahout pointed to their left; a rhinoceros was trying to step up the bank out of the river. It took four attempts, time for plenty of photographs to the delight of the four travellers. After a while, Jane got used to the motion and began to enjoy herself. She became aware of Mike's thigh next to her own. Since they were both wearing shorts it was a skin-to-skin sensation.

'I've changed my mind,' she said quietly to Mike. 'I want this to go on forever.' He grinned and held her arm closer.

After the ride had come to an end, much to the regret of Mike and Jane, they went with the rest of the party to see the elephants being washed in the river. As the mahouts lead them into the water, they took water into their trunks and sprayed it over themselves and anyone else who was in the vicinity. There was a great deal of laughter and splashing, and both Jane and Mike were soaked.

'The wet t-shirt look suits you, Jane.'

'Well it feels a bit uncomfortable. I think I'll go back to the lodge for a shower.'

'Good plan, I'll join you if that's alright.' They walked slowly back to the lodge. Mike followed Jane to her room and shut the door. The room was in dappled shade, the bed had been freshly made, the shutters were closed. Most of the other guests were out for various tourist activities so it seemed as if they were alone.

'What are we doing Mike, is this is good idea?'

'It's the best idea I've had for years.' He drew her towards him and kissed her eyes, then her mouth.

'Perhaps you should take that wet t-shirt off, I'll help you.' He took off his own shirt and held her close, their wet, clammy skin sticking them together. When they pulled apart there was a slurping sound. Jane giggled. They took off their shorts and lay on the cool sheets. A breeze came through the shutters.

'I never thought this would be happening to me, Mike.'

'Are you pleased it is?' She turned to kiss him as her answer.

Hours later, they joined the rest of the group for dinner. They were all talking about the elephant safari and showing each other the photographs they had taken. Max had sat on an elephant while it was being washed and had been moved to tears. They joked that he had probably just got water on his cheeks although they all understood what he meant. There was a brief pause in the repartee as Mike and Jane joined them. Jane felt her face go warm.

'Great wasn't it,' said Mike. 'Shame that Caroline and Sandra missed it.'

'Have you heard from them? When are they coming here?' asked David.

'No contact at the moment. There may be no signal where they are.'

Despite the slight coolness from the rest of the group, Jane and Mike sat close together over dinner. They sat around with the group for a short while with a drink after dinner, then first Jane and a short while later, Mike, slipped away.

Chapter 8
ANOTHER WORLD

After several hours of trekking, Caroline, Sandra and their guide arrived at the village. In contrast to the happy playing children they had seen only the previous day, there were a few children crying while others were just sitting quietly. The teacher was nowhere to be seen.

'Whatever has happened, where's the teacher?' Their guide went over to one of the groups of children to ask. The children, all speaking at once, tried to explain. Caroline and Sandra sat down on a school bench. When the guide came back to explain he looked distressed.

'One of the older girls has been taken,' he explained.

'What do you mean?' asked Caroline.

'Children are regularly abducted, either for ransom or for the night entertainment industry in Kathmandu or other towns,' explained Sandra.

'Oh my God,' said Caroline. 'How did it happen?'

'The school bus was stopped and two men took the girl away,' said the guide.

'Where's the teacher?' asked Sandra.

'She has gone to the next village to tell the police. She should be back soon.'

'What about the children?' asked Caroline.

'I have to get going back to Pokhara,' said the guide. 'What are you going to do?'

'We can't leave these kids,' said Sandra. 'We will stay here until their teacher comes back.'

The guide looked doubtful. 'Well how will you get back? You can't walk back in the dark.'

'We'll have to stay here then,' said Caroline. She knew that she sounded more confident than she felt.

'We have a trekking group coming through the village tomorrow so you can join them to get back to your hotel. I'll let them know so they'll be expecting you.'

'We'll do that. Thank you.'

'Let's go and talk to the kids,' said Sandra.

The children had been staring at them. They were looking very serious as the women joined them. Sandra still had some pencils and paper in her bag. She got them out and handed them around. The children were dressed in their western-looking school uniforms and Caroline was impressed by how clean and ordered they looked in contrast to their surroundings. She could feel a lump in her throat and hoped that she could hold back her tears. Sandra seemed to be in her element engaging with the children. Caroline envied her confidence.

'What shall I do, Sandra?' she asked.

'Just smile and talk to them. They've had a fright and since they've come a long way to get to school we should help make them feel it was worth it. It doesn't take much for them to stop coming. Some parents are more than happy if they give up school so that they can be unpaid labour.' Caroline shook herself and straightened her back.

'It's bloody awful,' she said. 'What chance do these children have?'

Sandra didn't bother to reply since the answer was perfectly clear.

Between them, they encouraged the children to go into the school room and sit around the tables which served as desks. In a rickety old cupboard there were a few books.

'Let's get them to sing us a song,' said Sandra. 'We can't do much else.'

'I hope the teacher comes back soon,' said Caroline.

By the time the teacher returned, the children had sung several songs and the crying had stopped. Caroline was beginning to feel confident, to enjoy being with the children. Sandra explained that their guide had left and they had decided to stay with the children.

'Have you any news about the girl?' asked Caroline.

'No, this is the third time this has happened this month and the police don't seem to be able to stop it. There's not enough of them and there are so many villages that need to be policed. Some children travel long distances to get to school. It can be a dangerous journey.'

'What time will school finish today?' asked Sandra.

'Six o'clock, the same as usual,' said the teacher. 'They mustn't make the journey for nothing.'

'Is there anything we can do?' asked Caroline.

'Won't you need to be getting back to Pokhara?'

'Our guide has already gone, so we will join a trekking group tomorrow,' said Sandra. 'So we have some time.' The teacher got out an old faded chart with pictures of taps and water on it.

'This is part of our attempt to teach about the need for washing and hygiene,' she explained. Caroline's face paled as the implications dawned on her. Facilities in the hotels weren't brilliant. What they were like in the villages she dreaded to think.

Just before six o'clock there was the sound of an old vehicle slowing down to stop outside the school. The teacher ended the school day and most of the children went outside to get into the bus. Caroline was relieved to see that there were two men in uniform. There would be no repeat abduction on the way home. Not all the children were going home by bus, some had a few miles to walk. The teacher told them not to accept lifts from drivers even if that meant they got home later. None of the children were fat and Carol could see why; they lead very physically demanding lives.

'We have to stay in the village tonight,' said Sandra. 'Do you know if there is anywhere we can have some food and beds for the night?'

'I will be happy if you stay with me. I live here in the village with my parents and sisters.'

'Thank you,' said Caroline. It had seemed a good idea to come back to the school but she hadn't planned on having to stay in the village and was glad that Sandra was with her.

'My name is Bihana. You are welcome in our house,' said the teacher. Caroline and Sandra walked slowly with her to the family house, which was a short distance away. It was built of stone with a tin roof and enlivened by painted blue shutters. There was a stone-paved courtyard which contained the cooking stove; this was just three large flat stones surrounding burning wood. The smoke made Caroline cough and her eyes run. Bihana took them into the house, which was dark and cool. The rest of the family were in and out preparing vegetables for the evening meal.

'We have no indoor toilet. I am sorry.'

'That's OK,' said Sandra. Caroline's face flushed. She told herself that she needed to be adaptable. The trek had been good preparation. The family made a meal, which she ate with an appetite that surprised her. Bihana gave up her room for Caroline and Sandra, and shared her sisters' room. When it was dark, Caroline went outside. She wandered around looking for what could be the outside toilet. On her way back to the house, she tripped over a stone step and fell. Her landing was soft and muddy. Her sharp, elegant knee-length shorts were ruined.

Back in the light inside the house, she tried to clean them up.

'Let me take them,' said Bihana. 'I will wash them, they will be dry by the time you leave tomorrow. I can give you something to wear.' She got out from a carved wooden cupboard a small pile of soft clothes.

'Do take these.' Caroline took off her own soiled clothes and put on a pair of thin, cotton, purple trousers and a pink long shirt. There was also a large purple scarf. Bihana showed her how to drape it around her neck and shoulders.

'It suits you, Caroline,' said Sandra. 'It's called a kurta.'

'I love it,' said Caroline. 'It feels so comfortable and light.' The women in the house clapped and laughed. The younger sister got out a beaded necklace and a pewter bangle and passed it shyly to Caroline.

'Thank you so much, it's all beautiful,' she said with a lump in her throat.

When Caroline and Sandra were eventually alone in their room she began to cry.

Sandra said nothing, asked no questions and put her arms around her. In a while the tears stopped and Caroline moved out of the embrace.

'I feel so confused. Excited and happy all at the same time.'

Chapter 9
FAMILY ENCUMBRANCES

The next morning, Caroline and Sandra joined up with a trekking group when they passed through the village and, after a few hours of walking, took the bus with them to Pokhara and their hotel. Later in the evening, Caroline received a text from Vishnu who had arranged their transport to Chitwen National Park for the following day. She wore the kurta for comfort. During the journey to Chitwen, Sandra occupied herself by writing in her diary. Caroline looked out of the window and thought about what she had experienced during the previous twenty-four hours.

After a long, tiring journey, they arrived at the lodge to join the rest of their group. They were sitting around in the bar having cool drinks and talking about their river trip in a dug-out canoe. They were excited. A crocodile had taken a dog from the village so to a few of them the canoe ride had seemed dangerous, "on the edge", as David put it. When Caroline and Sandra walked into the room the conversation stopped.

'Welcome back ladies,' said David. 'Caroline you look great, have you gone native?'

Mike, who was sitting with Jane, got up to greet them.

'Glad you're back. We were getting a bit concerned. Vishnu told us what had happened. Poor you. Are you alright Caroline? You look different.'

'It's probably these clothes. Bihana, the school teacher, gave them to me when I ruined my shorts. I will give it back to her when I next see her.'

'It's a kurta,' said Sandra. 'I love the bright colours, a bit of a change from Surrey lady shorts.'

'Much more comfortable,' said Caroline with a smile.

'Let me get you both a drink,' said Mike. 'Then you can tell me all about it.'

'I'm rather tired Mike and I could do with a shower, so I'll go to our room and see you later. No need to rush, I don't want to spoil your plans for the evening.'

Caroline and Sandra checked in to the lodge and went to their rooms.

After a shower and a change of clothes, Caroline sat on the bed. Although she was tired there was too much to think about to even consider sleep. It was impossible to ignore the frisson between Mike and Jane. She didn't enjoy watching his longing. Only a few more days then they would be leaving Nepal. After about an hour, the door to their room opened.

'How are you now, recovered?'

'I'm fine now, thanks. Has it been good?'

'Yes, elephant rides and so on. Just like it said in the brochure.'

'There's a bit more than that though, isn't there?' Mike didn't reply.

'Let me pour you a glass of wine. There's something we need to talk about.' She noticed that there was a half-drunk bottle of white wine on the table. 'I'm afraid it's not chilled.'

He poured them each a glass of wine and sat down in the only armchair in the room.

'While you've been away, I've heard from our son. He's decided that he's leaving uni. He says that he doesn't know what he wants to do and that it's a waste of his time and money to carry on.'

'What did you say?'

'I told him to think about it, don't make a rash decision that you might live to regret. He agreed to give it a few weeks until the end of term. What do you make of it?'

'A few weeks ago I would have been dead against it. But now, after being here, I'm not so sure.'

'I asked him what he was going to do instead and he said that he didn't know yet.' The implications of Oliver's potential decision began to dawn on Caroline. She felt her heart sink.

'Just so long as he doesn't want to come home to live. I've done being the home maker.'

'Where else can he go?'

'It's not my problem. I am not going to feel obliged to accommodate him.'

'What's happening to you? You're talking about our son.'

'I'm talking about my own wishes for once.'

'I'm going back to join the others. We can talk about it when we get home. He will probably have changed his mind by then.'

'Well I won't have changed mine.' Mike shut the door with more force than was strictly necessary. When he had gone, Caroline got up and went to see Sandra. She knocked on her door. There was no immediate answer, so she stood quietly wondering what to do. There was the sound of crying, she knocked again. When there was again no response, she went back to her own room, quickly undressed and got into bed.

I'm glad it's a single bed, was her brief thought. *I just don't want to sleep with Mike.*

She heard him come to bed. When she looked at her watch it was 2 am. He undressed quietly in the dark and she pretended to be asleep. *What a cliché. How has it come to this?* To her surprise, although she felt distressed, she began to see it as the first steps towards the next phase in her life.

At breakfast the next morning, Sandra chatted to the other members of the group about the plans for the day. Caroline wondered whether she had imagined the sound of her crying. When she looked closely she could see that her eyes looked a bit inflamed and puffy.

Caroline joined the table and tried to enter into the spirit of the group. The day had been designated as a free day after the previous hectic, action-packed days. Most of the group were planning to sit in the lovely lodge grounds and either swim in the pool or read and generally take it easy.

Vishnu had offered to arrange for Sandra and Caroline to go on the elephant safari. Neither of them were in the mood for it so they thanked him and declined the offer.

'Sandra, can I have a word?' asked Caroline.

'Let's have a gentle walk around the gardens after breakfast.'

Mike had not appeared for breakfast, neither had Jane. When they were all present, Caroline felt that the group atmosphere moved into uncomfortable.

When Sandra got up from the table, she nodded at Caroline who moved to join her. They didn't speak until they were away from the lodge.

'Is everything alright, Sandra?'

'Not really. I had a phone call with my son. My grandson is still in hospital having tests. He has a chest infection, which is taking longer than usual to clear.' Caroline made a sympathetic response. Sandra continued, 'He wants me to come home. I don't understand his reasons. I'm not a doctor, there's nothing I can do.'

'Perhaps he just wants moral support.'

'No doubt – and I want my life. I'm not going to live forever, I want some me time. I find the sense of obligation that they want me to feel is a negative force in my life. I feel oppressed by it.' Caroline nodded in agreement.

'So what will you do?'

'I am not going back.'

'That's very brave. It's not easy to go against the expectations of the family.'

'I know, but I've given in for too long. I resent it and that's not good for anybody. They are going to have to learn that I'm not just a mother and grandmother, but someone with needs and values of my own.'

'So what are you going to do?'

'Stay in Nepal and build a life for myself here, at least for the time being. If I go back the family will take over my life again.' Caroline put her arm around her shoulders.

'Good for you. Sometimes we need to put distance between ourselves and our families or be overwhelmed by them.'

'I'll never be without the guilt, but I'll just have to manage that. It's a price that I'm prepared to pay.' They walked on together without speaking. Caroline knew that it was not the right time to discuss her own dilemma about Oliver and all the other issues occupying her mind. She wanted to be there as a support for Sandra. That was a responsibility that she had willingly chosen, it hadn't just crept up on her like most of the other encumbrances in her life.

When they returned to the lodge, Mike and Jane were sitting together having a late breakfast. To Caroline they looked comfortable and pleased to be together. Jane looked as if the last few days had been a tonic, a world away from the pale and sickly woman she had been in the first few days.

'Good morning,' said Caroline. 'Have you any plans for the day?'

'I was waiting to see what you wanted to do,' said Mike.

'I'm planning to have a chat with Vishnu about the school,' said Caroline. 'So I'll be busy. You go off and have a nice time. I'll see you around this evening.' She noticed the relief on Mike's face and the pleasure she felt on deciding her own agenda.

Chapter 10
TIME TO MOVE ON?

The last day of the holiday dawned. The sky was overcast. Caroline dragged herself out of bed after a restless night. Mike had already got up and dressed and gone down to breakfast. She knew that when she appeared he would be sitting with Jane. The tears came, slowly at first and then faster until she was crying like a woman bereft. In a while she had run out of emotion and stopped crying. There was a knock on the door.

'Caroline are you alright. Are you coming down for breakfast? They'll stop serving it soon,' said Sandra. Caroline opened the door. When Sandra saw her blotchy, puffy face, she wrapped her arms around her and held her tight.

'Thank you. That's just what I need. There's too much happening. I can't cope with it.'

'I'll bring us up some coffee and toast and we can have breakfast here in your room if you like.'

By the time Sandra returned with their breakfast on a tray, Caroline had splashed cold water on her face and looked more like her collected self. They ate the toast in silence, a comforting silence.

'I wonder what has happened to the girl, the one who was abducted. I was thinking about her in the night,' said Caroline.

'We could ask Vishnu to find out,' replied Sandra.

'We have to get real Sandra. It's no good being romantic about it. What can we do in Nepal?'

'Well we won't know unless we try.'

'I have such mixed feelings about Mike. I know in my head that I need to move on in some way or another, but it's hard to see him so engaged with Jane. I should be pleased for him and it makes it easier for me. It's just so painful to let go.'

'Of course it is. Change always comes with some losses as well as gains. That's why it is difficult. Many people won't even allow themselves to contemplate it. You've been brave to get this far.' A mobile phone rang. Caroline picked it up from the bedside table.

'It's Oliver, my son. I need to answer it.'

'OK, I'll see you downstairs when you're ready. We will talk to Vishnu about the girl.'

'Thank you,' said Caroline as she picked up the phone. 'Hello Oliver, lovely to hear from you.'

Ten minutes later after the conversation with Oliver, Caroline put the phone down with a sigh. After checking her face in the mirror and combing her hair, she picked up her phone and went down to the dining room to find Mike.

As she expected, he was sitting with Jane.

'Mike, I need a word. I just had a chat with Oliver.'

'Is he alright?'

'Not really. Can we just talk in private?'

'Of course. Sorry Caroline. Shall we go up to our room?'

'No. Let's just go outside.' Mike got up, leaving his

unfinished breakfast and walked with Caroline into the grounds of the lodge.

'It's not good Mike. Oliver has to leave uni.'

'Why, what's he done?'

'He's got a drug dependency problem. Diazepam, he's been taking it to stop his anxiety. Otherwise he can't sleep, so he says.'

'Bloody hell,' said Mike. 'How did that happen?'

'He's not the only one. They are under a lot of pressure.'

'I suppose so. What happens now?'

'He's seeing the college counsellor, there is student support. But he wants to come home.'

'Of course, that's the best thing for him,' said Mike.

'I'm not so sure about that. If he's getting professional support it might be better if he finishes the term. Otherwise he'll have to repeat the year.'

'What did you say to him Caroline?'

'Not a lot, I mostly listened. Eventually I said that we would be home in a few days. I urged him not to do anything rash. I could do without this Mike. I thought the children had left home and we could get on with our own lives.' Mike gave her a hug.

'Well we can't do any more until we get home.' They walked slowly back to the lodge. Mike kicked at stones in the gravel path.

'This holiday has not turned out in the way we expected,' said Caroline.

'Too bloody true, I'm still glad I came though. Are you?' Caroline paused to think before she replied.

'Yes I am. We need to get real. We've been avoiding it

for some time. Go and finish your breakfast Mike. I need to have a word with Sandra.'

The climax of the final evening of the holiday was a party with Vishnu and the sherpas at the trekking centre. The group gathered at the front of the lodge to wait for the minibus. They had all made an effort to spruce themselves up for their final evening together. Caroline wore the purple and pink kurta with the bracelet and necklace.

'I'm making a statement,' she explained to Sandra.
'Which is?' said Sandra.
'This is a new me. I know Mike likes me to wear elegant clothes. I'm fed up with it. This is more comfortable. I don't have to worry if my skirt is too short or too tight so I can focus on more important stuff.' Sandra agreed. She was wearing her usual flowing skirt and a colourful scarf around her shoulders.

'I've bought myself these silver earrings.'
'They look good with your silver streaks in your hair,' said Caroline. The men had also made an effort to look smart. Mike wore a crisp white shirt, which showed off his broad shoulders and tanned face. They got into the minibus to be driven to the trekking centre.

'I'll sit with Sandra,' said Caroline. Mike sat with Jane.

The trekking centre had been decorated for the party with flags and coloured lights which were strung between the trees. There was a dinner, this time not cooked by the sherpas but for them. At the end of the meal, a huge cake was produced and Vishnu made a speech followed by enthusiastic applause. Then there was music and dancing in the garden. David asked Caroline to join him in the dancing. In a dark corner, he tried to kiss her.

'You look wonderful Caroline, interesting and exotic. What's been going on with you and Mike and Jane?'

'Holidays and foreign places can have strange effects on people you know.'

'I know what you mean,' he said. 'Dangerous stuff.' Caroline smiled.

'Mike must be mad to want Jane when he's got you. Who wants water when they can have champagne?'

'I'll take that as a compliment, David. But he hasn't "got me" as you put it. Well not anymore. I'm starting to be my own woman. That means that however nice you are, for the present, that's not where I'm going.'

'What a shame,' said David as he twirled her around to the music. 'But good for you.'

'Can we take a break David, I'm hot and I could do with some water and a glass of white wine.' They walked over to where a bar had been set up. Sitting at a table alone were Mike and Jane. They were deep in conversation and Caroline felt a lump in her throat as she observed how attentive Mike was being to her. Jane was wearing a dress that would be described as demure. She looked pretty and feminine and gazed lovingly at Mike. He didn't notice Caroline and David approaching.

'Can we join you?' asked David. Mike looked up, startled when he saw Caroline.

'Of course,' he said and got up to fetch a chair for Caroline while David moved a chair for himself from the next empty table. Mike recovered his cool and offered to go to the bar to get the drinks.

'Having a good time Jane?' asked David.

Caroline thought that it sounded aggressive so she said, 'I like your dress, Jane. The flowers are pretty.' Jane smiled a thank you and then the three of them sat in silence listening to the music. They were all glad when Mike returned with the drinks.

'Have you enjoyed the trip, Mike?' asked David. 'It must have been disappointing that you couldn't finish the trek.'

'Of course,' said Mike. 'Despite that I wouldn't have missed it. A fascinating country. Shame your wife didn't come with you.'

'She wouldn't have enjoyed it,' said David. 'How about you, Jane?'

'It's been lovely,' said Jane, her face flushing. She stood up. 'I'll just go and sit with Sandra, she's by herself.'

David stood up and began moving around to the music.

'I'll join the dancing,' he said and wandered off carrying his glass of beer. Caroline and Mike moved their chairs closer together so they could hear each other speak above the music.

'Jane seems like a good woman,' said Caroline.

'I think she needs looking after,' said Mike. 'She's on her own now and she's not strong like you are.'

'You are good at doing that, Mike. You've looked after the children and me and I'm grateful.' Mike took a long drink of his beer.

'I've been happy to do it, Caroline.'

'I don't need it any longer. I don't want to be dependent on you, or anyone else for that matter.'

'I can see that. This has been developing for a while.'

'I suppose it has. This trip has just made it clearer.' She sipped her wine. 'Here's Jane.' Mike got up and placed a chair for her next to his.

'Where's Sandra?' asked Caroline.

'She's talking to Vishnu about the girl who was abducted.'

'I think I'll join her,' said Caroline. 'See you later Mike.' She realised that she still felt possessive about him.

Sandra and Vishnu were sitting well away from the noise and festivities when Caroline joined them. Sandra looked up.

'It's not good news. The girl is still missing.'

Chapter 11
OPPORTUNITIES AND THREATS

Mike zipped up his travel bag.

'I've finished my packing. Do you need any help?'

'Could you help me squash this into my bag? I've bought quite a lot of stuff. I love these cushions with elephants on them.'

'In a few hours we will be on the plane back to London,' said Mike. 'How do you feel about that Caroline?'

'That's a good question. Confused I suppose. A lot has happened in a short time, I'm still getting used to things.'

'What in particular?'

'Well, us for a start. We can't carry on as if nothing has happened.'

'I suppose not. What do you suggest?'

'I've been thinking about it Mike. I want to come back to Nepal and see if I can do something useful. You seem to have started a relationship with Jane. Why don't you see if that works out?'

'Do you mean you want us to separate?'

'Since I plan to come back to Nepal for a while, maybe we could just allow each other to live our own lives for a while to see if it's what we really want.'

'What about the children, what if Oliver leaves uni?'

'They aren't children anymore. I can't give up anymore of my life. He'll have to sort it out for himself. You'll be there for him.'

'Are you sure about this?'

'The only thing that I'm sure of is that I have to give myself a chance. We've had a good life together but I feel as if I don't exist in my own right: I'm your wife, Oliver's mother. It's not enough now.'

Mike tried hard but couldn't hold back his tears. He held out his arms.

'I can't bear the thought of losing you. You're part of my life.'

'We can't have everything Mike. We have to make choices and compromises. I think we are both ready for something new and different. I know it won't be easy, but I know we have to give it a try. Well I know I have to.'

'Then I suppose I have to let you go, if that's what you want.'

At Khatmandu Airport the trekking group stood around waiting for their flight, which was, as expected, delayed by several hours. They were exchanging phone numbers and email addresses and promising to stay in touch. Those who were experienced travellers knew that it was unlikely. Sandra had come with them to the airport to say goodbye.

'I'm not coming back,' she told Caroline. 'There will be too much emotional blackmail. I would give in.'

'I'll email you when I make my arrangements to come back,' said Caroline. 'Please stay in touch. I may need some support and encouragement.'

'Of course,' said Sandra. 'But I think you'll be fine, you've moved on.'

Mike and Jane stood quietly together. Caroline put her arms around them.

'Cheer up you two, it's only the end of the holiday, not the end of the world.' Jane tried to smile and only just managed it

'It wasn't what I expected,' she whispered.

'In what way?' asked Caroline.

'In every way. Nepal for a start, it's been a culture shock to say the least. But the biggest shock is what I've discovered about myself.' Caroline nodded in encouragement. 'I thought I wanted to be independent now I don't have to care for my mother. I don't. I need to care for somebody. I don't want to be by myself. I want to be needed.' She wiped tears away. 'I'm dreading going back to an empty house. Being with the group has been like family.'

'You don't have to go back to an empty house,' said Caroline. 'There's plenty of room in our house, it's too big now the children have left home. You could come and stay while we all work out what to do.' There was a moment's silence as Mike took a deep breath.

'That's alright with you isn't it, Mike?' asked Caroline. There was a missed beat before he said 'Yes of course. A bloody good idea.'

On the flight home, Carol and Mike sat together according to their ticket designations. Jane sat several rows in front of them next to an empty seat which had been Sandra's. Caroline felt a stab of loneliness.

Her understanding and support had been a great help, 'I miss Sandra,' she said. 'She understands.'

'I'm trying to,' said Mike, 'but it's hard. You seem different, not my dear old Caroline.'

'Perhaps this is the real me. I need to find out.'

An hour into the flight Caroline turned to Mike, 'Why don't you go and sit next to Jane for a while. I could do with a nap.'

'Are you sure?'

'Yes.'

He got up and went to sit next to Jane. Caroline saw their heads close together as they talked quietly. She felt a lump in her throat and saw clearly that she was about to give up something special. Was it worth it? Only time would tell. She put her sunglasses on to hide her tears. She took the purple scarf that Bihana had given to her out of her rucksack and folded it up to make a pillow. She had said that she would return it. She wasn't going to break her promise.